THE CROCODILE'S SON

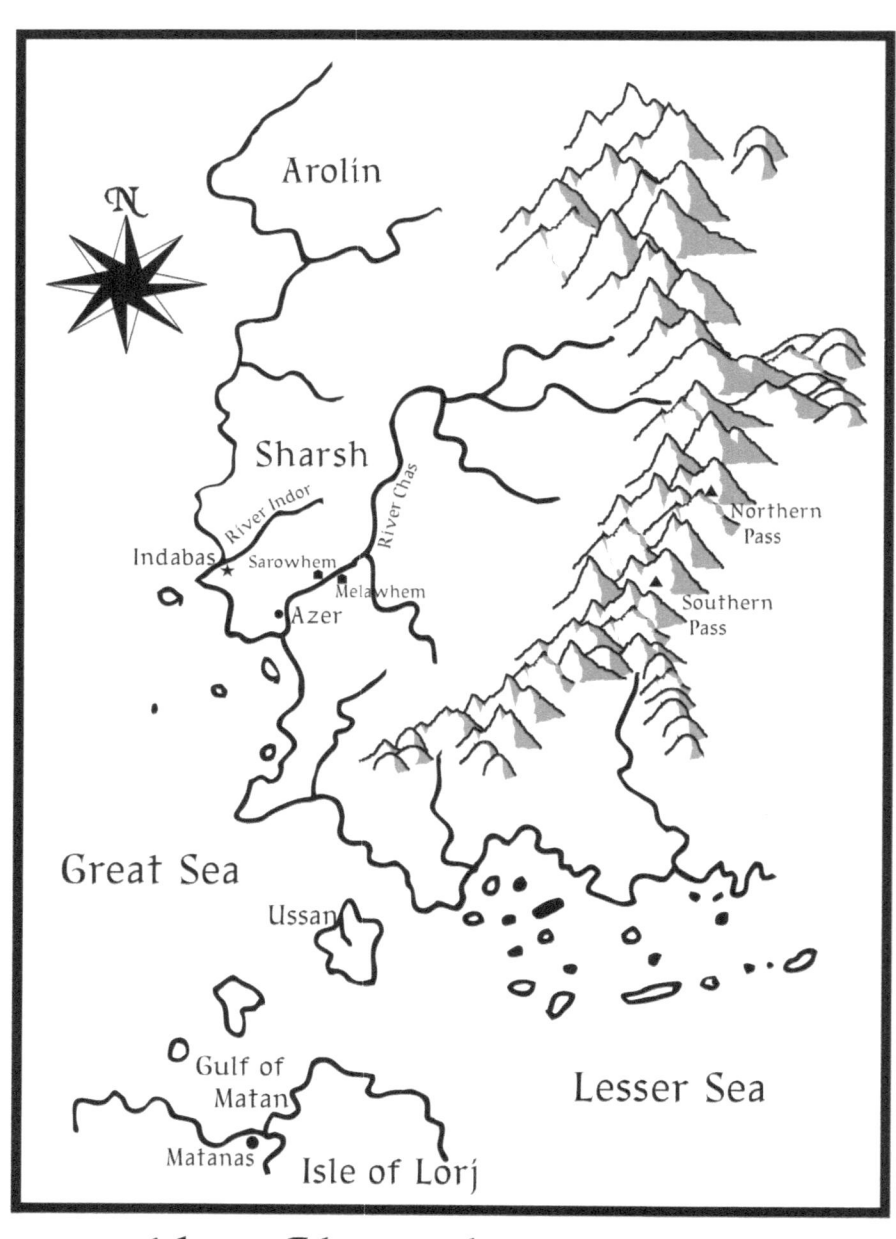

the Sharsh of Qala

The Crocodile's Son

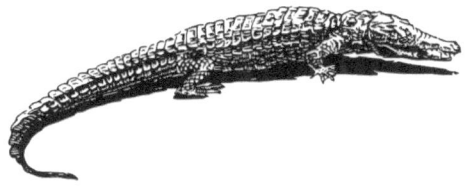

Stephen Brooke

Arachis Press 2017

*Monster and god in each of us, and who is to say
which will have its victory at the last?*

The Crocodile's Son
©2017 Stephen Brooke

ISBN 978-1-937745-42-4

Arachis Press
4803 Peanut Road
Graceville, FL 32440
http://arachispress.com

Part I.
THE PREGNANT PIRATE

1.

"So you are telling me that my little Xit was, in fact, a god?"

"That is how it seems, my lady," answered Corad. The tall Sharshite nobleman sounded as though he himself found it hard to believe. "My sister says his true name is Xido. Xido the Trickster."

"Well, he was certainly a trickster," admitted Qala. "And he could turn into a crocodile, too? I should have remained in Azer a few more days and seen that!"

Corad hoped to never see a reptile so gigantic again but said nothing of that to his companion. Rather, he asked, "Is he the father? If you do not mind me asking."

"Most likely. It is becoming noticeable, isn't it?" Qala was a small and slender woman, and her pregnancy, though not far along, was fairly obvious. "I do suppose the Admiral could be responsible. Either one is fine with me, I would have to say, though both are rather ugly!"

Corad laughed. "I am afraid I have to agree, my lady. Let us hope the child takes after you."

"I only hope he can't change into a crocodile," came Qala's reply.

"I'll drink to that," said Corad, raising his tankard. The bitter ale was not good but he drank deeply of it. The man was enjoying all things after his three years of captivity, slaving at the oars of a pirate galley. That the woman across the table from him was in some part responsible for that slavery, he did not hold against her.

Indeed, Corad considered the former pirate queen a friend. He looked about the inn's small common room. "Do you intend to stay here through the Yule?" he asked.

"You know we Mura don't celebrate that day as do your people. Our new year is in the spring." She sipped at her watered wine. "But yes, my villa is in no way ready for me to move in."

"Then come back to Sarowhem with me. You are welcome to share our Yule feast. After all," he pointed out, "we are practically neighbors now."

"Your parents would never think to invite one such as I, even knowing nothing of my past. This I know is true."

"Probably so. But you would be my guest, my lady."

"Very well, my Lord Corad," Qala spoke, "I shall accompany you home." She smirked at the Sharshite. "Shall we tell your parents I am your new bride?"

"Oh, most certainly! And that it is my child you carry, eh?" Both chuckled.

"My road here led past Sarowhem," Qala told him. "I did not stop, as all your family was still in Azer for your sister's wedding. I must say, your father needs higher walls. I could take the place with half a dozen fighting men. And they needn't be good fighting men."

Corad nodded. "This is true. I have seen enough to convince me of the need for more defenses. And Marana's husband believes there is great trouble and turmoil coming."

"Saj sees things others can not."

"Yes. The two are better off in Lorj, I suppose, though I hated to see them leave."

"Any word?"

"Nay, it is too soon for a letter to make it back. I am sure Marana will write. Perhaps to you, my lady."

Qala sighed. "I doubt I would ever write back. I must depend on you to keep me up to date."

"So," said Corad, "we shall have visit each other from time to time. 'Tis only half a day's ride, after all."

"Then we shall make that ride in the morning, sir," said Qala, rising. "I shall be ready to depart at dawn."

Corad sat and drank a while after the Muram woman had left for her room and bed. He liked Qala, or thought he did, despite her past. And they had been comrades-in-arms, which counted for something. That she cared not for men, for the most part, was all to the good. It simplified matters.

One man after another slipped out into the dark, leaving at last only Corad and the innkeeper. "May I, sir?" the man asked, pulling out a chair. Corad nodded. "You are a friend of the Lady Qala, my lord?"

"That I am. We, ah, sailed together." Having someone like Qala as a guest here would be unusual. This rustic little inn was unlikely to have many guests at all. "I trust you are not overcharging her."

"Oh, I am not charging her at all! She owns this inn, sir. She owns this town. We did not know this when she arrived, having always dealt with her agents before." The man grinned. "The ferryman tried to cheat her when she wished to cross over to her villa. She had great fun haggling with him before she fired the fellow! Good riddance, I say." He nodded his head in approval. "It will be good to have someone in residence here again."

"Ha, had I known this I would have expected to drink for free!"

"Unlikely to happen, sir. She is a woman of business, I could see that right away. Made her fortune on the seas, did she?"

"Indeed she did." Best he say no more about that. "I'll not gossip about her, my good man. The Lady Qala will reveal what she wishes."

"Oh, aye, sir. Understood. We're all curious about her, of course."

"Of course. I'm for my bed. The lady and I are departing early. See that our mounts are ready."

2.

"I realized I was with child by the time I arrived at my estate," said Qala, as the pair rode westward along the banks of the broad River Chas. To their right lay the faded brown fields of mid-winter, and the gray forest beyond. "I have been pregnant before but ended it. A pirate queen in such condition would not long have held her throne.

"A pirate queen in exile is another matter and I am not young anymore nor likely to have another chance. So there will be an heir to my estates, it seems."

"My parents are already urging me to marry and provide an heir too," stated Corad. "I do not think I am quite ready to go back into servitude so soon!"

"Had you not been among our rowers, you would have been married by now, no?"

"That is likely, my lady. But I shall not thank you for it." They rode on without speaking for a few minutes before he commented, "You have become a good rider."

"Thanks to this gentle pony. I had not ridden since I was a girl." She patted her mount's neck. "I have named him Jacef."

"After your second in command?" The man she had slain during their escape from the pirate stronghold — it seemed an odd choice to Corad.

"Why, you wonder? Because it is the gelding I should have made of him!" Qala snickered at her joke. "My journey upriver was easy and I soon became accustomed to riding again. I had little enough to take with me, you know, a few odds and ends I purchased in Azer. The cart my attendant drove behind me was mostly empty!"

"It was a good idea to have a man with you, none the less," opined the Sharshite. "It discourages trouble."

Qala laughed. "You know I am quite capable to taking care of myself should any trouble have arisen along the way. But I suppose having a lackey does help and I felt I needed to make a good appearance, hence the wagon and attendant. At any rate, my journey was without incident."

She seemed to gather her thoughts for a few seconds before continuing. "I might have welcomed an incident or two to relieve the boredom of my ride, had I not been intrigued by all the little things I saw along the way. It has been so long since I was in the countryside, being confined to ships and my island stronghold as I was. The brief call at one seedy port or another hardly counts.

"As I rode, I saw hatred in many eyes. Hatred for the Mura and for the wealthy, and I am both! Only a few months ago I would have had men flogged for giving me such looks. Other men gave me other sorts of looks but those mean little to me."

"I think those are to be expected, my lady."

Qala shrugged. "I am not sure why men give me such looks. I am little and shriveled up and have no beauty of face. Nor am I very young anymore. This did not keep me from eyeing the pretty girls, myself. Aye, or the occasional young lad. I can admit to that. But I did no more than look. I intend to be well settled in my new home before getting into any trouble of that sort."

"Hmm, well, you are small," admitted Corad, "and Muram to boot. But the same things could be said of my brother-in-law. And, my lady," he added, "you are considerably better looking."

"Your sister did not think so!"

Best Qala never know how close Marana had come to giving herself to her, thought Corad. Best not even think about how differently things might have turned out. Or, as Xit claimed, could they have turned out no other way?

"These mark the boundaries of my family's estate," stated Corad, as they passed between head-high posts on either side of their path. "We should be at the villa before the noon."

"Sarowhem. I should have a name for my place!"

"It means nothing more than the house of Saros, in the Sharshic lan-

9

guage, that being our family name. Have you such a name you might use, Lady Qala?"

"Not one that would make any sense to you Sharshites." She laughed and continued. "Qala isn't even my real name. It means 'queen' in my native dialect."

"Oh. Yes, I see that. Not so different from the form in Imperial Muram. I believe you are the only queen I have ever met. I have rarely even heard the word used," Corad told her. "The emperor does not approve of claimants to a royal title."

"Plenty of them across the Greater Sea. Too many."

The nobleman nodded. "And forever warring on each other." He raised a hand in greeting to a burly farmhand they passed.

I must remember to be more friendly toward my underlings, Qala told herself. She knew it would not come natural to her. "I think I shall obtain a boat," she announced, looking toward the wide waterway to their left. "It would make it easier to visit."

Corad's expression was sour. "I have had quite enough of boats, my lady."

"I myself am done with the sea and hope never to smell salt upon the air again, but I am willing to sail upon this river." Qala looked out over the Chas for a few seconds. "Yes, I am done with that life forever. Whether that life is done with me, only the gods would know."

The road turned away from Chas as they neared Corad's ancestral home, for the villa lay directly upon the banks of the river, and the way must pass around it. The pair of travelers did not pass but stopped before the main gate. To their right, another road ran north toward the hills dividing the valleys of the Chas and the Indor.

Qala gazed up it. "That is the way Saj would have first come here, isn't it?"

"It is. It's a pretty decent road if you ever want to visit Indabas." Corad smiled broadly. "Without smelling the salt air."

"Indabas itself is on the ocean, young man, as you well know. I was there once on, ah, business. There is no reason to go back." Qala chuckled. "I've an agent who can deliver bribes."

"Is that needed, my lady?" asked Corad, dismounting. Grooms had promptly come forth to hold both horses. "I mean, now that you are retired?"

Qala slipped from her saddle. It was a good distance down for the petite pirate. "I needed to make sure my status as a citizen was unquestioned. Thanks to a small sum here and there and a good word from Admiral Murgom, I am officially acknowledged as a patrician of the empire." She took a moment to brush the dust from her riding gown. "That is enough title for me, I think."

In some respects, better than that of his father, thought Corad. Patrician was the only title that mattered to a Mur — one was either a citizen or a subject. "Well then, we must present you as such to the thegn. It is certainly a step up from the scullery maid you claimed to be on your first meeting!"

3.

Aside from a pair of servant women hanging laundry in the weak mid-winter sunlight, the courtyard was deserted. "Perhaps," began Qala, "we should let your parents believe what they will about who is, ah, responsible for my condition."

Corad agreed. "The admiral would be the natural assumption. They know nothing of your time with Xit." He paused and looked down at his companion. "Explaining your new station among the landed gentry might be more difficult."

Qala had hinted of having some money set aside when they had first landed at Azer. She would have to embroider on that. "I must be a wealthy widow," the pirate decided.

"That should work. We go in this way." The nobleman had turned aside from the tall double-doors standing opposite the gate. The main hall of Sarowhem followed a typical Sharshite architectural pattern, a high central part and lower side sections, with windows above. Behind it, rose other buildings, including a blocky two story edifice toward her right. Following Qala's eyes, Corad told her, "That's the living quarters. Over there," he said, nodding toward their left, "are the stables and docks."

He turned into a unobtrusive arched entryway, its plank door standing ajar. "Straight to the kitchens, this way," he announced. "Food before family!"

"They'll know you are here, won't they?"

"Someone will tell someone I arrived, sooner or later. They won't know who you are, of course. Hail, Master Lovi!" A sallow, heavy-set man looked up from whatever he was sauteing. Onions, it smelled like, but something else too, some pungent herb. Qala could not quite place it.

"You have a Muram cook?" she asked Corad.

"Indeed we do. My father hired him away from some inn down in Azer."

"That is correct, madame," said the man, squinting in her direction. "I was a sailor who decided one day to stay in port." His accent spoke of the kingdoms beyond the Great Sea. "Are you hungry, my lady? I can have something for the both of you in a minute or two."

"Don't bother," said the nobleman. "I know well where to find bread and cheese." He turned to ask Qala, "Wine or beer?"

"The beer is freshly brewed," Lovi informed him. "Shall I bring you some?" He looked from one to the other.

Qala nodded. "That would do," spoke Corad. The Muram cook bustled off to fetch it. "The family will be eating lunch in an hour or so," the Sharshite said, brushing flour from one of the trestle tables and offering his companion a seat on a bench. "And then siesta. We can do all our formal greetings after they wake up." The man kept his tone light, expressing something near amusement with his family. How different his life was now! "We might do well to nap first ourselves."

"A chance to rest and refresh would be welcome," agreed Qala. "We Mura don't do siestas, however."

"I know. You consider Sharshites terribly lazy." He brought a loaf and large wedge of pale cheese to the table and began slicing them, rather unevenly. A moment later, Lovi brought three flagons of pale beer and sat down with them.

Qala knew enough of Sharshites not to be surprised by this informality. Such casual relationships between master and servant would never happen in a Muram household. Yet at the same time they were stricter here about their sexes mixing familiarly. Muram women tended to do as they wished.

"You are of my homeland, my lady," spoke the cook.

"I am," she agreed, cautious enough to offer nothing more, and sampled her beer. A good long quaff would give her time to piece together a story in her head. Who better to spread such a tale than the master of the kitchens? "It is a fine brew, sir."

"Indeed so, Lovi," stated Corad. "You Mura have a way with beer."

"Wine grapes won't grow well in most of our cold nations," said Qala. "We work with what we have." She took a typical Muram pride in practicality. "They do have vineyards down around Tesra though, if I remember right." Qala sighed, perhaps a tad too theatrically. "It has been long since I saw the lands of my birth."

Lovi nodded, seemingly sympathetic, but addressed the nobleman. "I should make the first black beer of the season in a month or so, my lord," he informed him. It had to be admitted, the mention of that brew did actually bring a brief sense of nostalgia to Qala. She had not sampled the dark beer of spring since — well, since she had first set foot on a ship.

The woman said, simply, "I must visit again then." She should still be able to travel; the child in her was not that far along. Laying it on even thicker this time, Qala added, "If only my late husband could have accompanied me!"

Corad tried valiantly to keep a sympathetic look on his face. "Was he Muram, my lady?" he asked.

"No, a merchant from the southern isles. I would rather not speak of him, Lord Corad," she stated. Let others fill in the gaps in her story as they wished. Lovi's look of sympathy was not feigned. It made the for-mer pirate queen feel almost guilty. But only almost.

"Let us find a room for you," spoke Corad, rising. "My sister's should work. She is unlikely to reclaim it."

Marana's bedchamber? That did pique Qala's curiosity. She had to admit that any other interest in the Sharshite girl had faded away. As did most things.

4.

It seemed the young Marana had few interests beyond horses. Qala found evidence of little else in the second-story rooms the girl had once inhabited. A few books. The former pirate read well enough — at times there had been little more to entertain her in her lonely life. Some of the tomes were rather weighty for a young noblewoman to be reading, history and military theory and treatises on animal husbandry, but there was also a selection of lurid romances. Qala unrolled one of the latter but could make little sense of it. She went to the wide window and peered out over the courtyard. There was a good command of the front gate from this vantage.

Qala very much suspected Marana had chosen the rooms for that reason. She liked to stay atop whatever was going on. If Marana had taken the offer to become her lover — and to make Saj her eventual heir — the pair would have done well ruling over the pirates. But the noblewoman had chosen otherwise — in the end, that had proven best for everyone.

A rap at the door and, before she could answer it, a girl entered with a pitcher. "Clean water for you, m'lady," she said, with the distinct accent of the countryside, the accent Qala had heard everywhere at her new estate. The young woman might have grown up speaking Sharshic, not Muram.

The girl set her burden next to a ceramic basin, and placed the towels she had slung over her arm beside them. "Will you need anything more, ma'am?" she asked. "Help with freshening up?" Hmm, nice enough looking, wasn't she? Qala wouldn't mind at all if this young lady helped her with her bath. But no, there wasn't time for indulgence.

"That will be enough, miss," she told her. "Is everyone still asleep?"

"Pretty much, m'lady. You have time for a nap yourself." She performed some sort of clumsy curtsy and slipped out of the room. Qala splashed some water on herself, rinsing away the dust of her morning ride, and then stretched on the bed, atop the covers, intending only to rest a moment. She was rather surprised to see how low the sun lay in the sky when her eyes opened again.

And the door unlatched and unguarded — how lax she had become! At least she had a dagger ready at hand, on her belt. Qala considered that fact for a moment. It would not do to go armed when she greeted her hosts. She must conceal the blade somewhere on her. Ah, she would don the one long gown she had brought along and could hide it readily in her boot.

It was too bad Marana had been such a big horse of a girl. Qala would float in any of the clothes she had left behind in this room. She found the gown in her pack and hurriedly slipped into it. Silk, it was, and green, a luxury she had afforded herself when she first arrived in Azer. Qala had spread around a bit too much money those first days, perhaps, making up for a great deal of lost time. Time spent in a damp fortress on a rock island in a hidden lagoon, her wealth all but useless to her there.

She sat by the window and gazed out on the courtyard, and the encroaching shadow of its west wall. Southwest, she corrected herself. Someone would come and fetch her in time.

There wasn't much going on down there. Qala knew exceedingly little of farming but suspected that things were not very busy at the time of the winter solstice. She would have to learn these things, wouldn't she? Maybe she should borrow one of Marana's scrolls on agriculture!

"What a lovely dress, m'lady!" gushed the servant who let herself in. The same one as before — Qala found herself wondering just how large a staff served at Sarowhem and how large she would need herself. So much to learn.

"Thank you, miss," she said, rising from her place. "Have you a name?" She *was* a winsome girl.

"Domi, m'lady. Let me shutter up that window for you. It's getting cool out." For a moment Qala thought to stay her but decided not. It would make the girl feel she was doing her job properly and she could always open it back up later if she wished. Qala liked the fresh air here, the clean country air. Fastening the solid shutters and, moreover, pulling thick mud-colored drapes across the window, the girl nodded in approval of her cold-proofing and said, "I'm to take you on down if you're ready, ma'am."

"As ready as I shall ever be, Domi." Qala suddenly felt a twinge of apprehension about spending time with this family of noble Sharshites. Who was she but a street girl from the slums of a seedy port city, an overgrown urchin?

Ah well, she had chosen to become Sharshite herself, hadn't she? If she didn't want to play the part, Qala should have found an estate else-where, on Lorj, maybe, or even in Muradon itself. No, she told herself, it is a new life you need, where no one would ever know who you were. But you know you were a queen once and no backwater Sharshite nobles should intimidate you!

She followed the servant girl down a wide, well-worn stairway. It turned back on itself at a windowless landing, before opening into a side-aisle of the main hall. Qala was composed now, ready to greet the thegn and his family, to present herself as their equal. To be familiar.

She also decided to make no advances to Domi. That might be bad manners in a house where she was a guest.

.

5.

"We hope to find a good match for Corad. If those awful pirates hadn't gotten hold of him, we might have had grandchildren by now!"

Qala gave the young nobleman at her side a meaningful look — a look Lady Belema completely misinterpreted.

"Oh yes, my dear, you were their captive too, weren't you?" Corad's mother seemed sincerely sympathetic. "It must have been dreadful."

The Muram woman only nodded. In a way, she had been as much a captive as the lowest galley slave. "I would just as soon not speak of it, my lady," she said.

"Belema. Call me Belema. You are one of us now."

"That you are," agreed the thegn. "One of the landed gentry." There was a tone of good-natured mockery in his voice, perhaps directed as much at himself as anyone.

"And a noble lady," Corad added, "whether you wish it or no. You should make certain that all address you as such in your new home."

"Oh, I've already put the fear of their new mistress into them!" replied Qala, laughing. "Speaking of matches, some of the farm girls there were sniffing about at an eligible nobleman when you stopped by, Corad."

"There are quite enough of those around here," allowed Lord Hur-rum. He turned his eyes to his guest. "Perhaps we need find a match for you as well, Qala."

"Maybe in time," was her answer. "There will be far too many things requiring my attention for a while." They would interpret that as they would. She took a bite of the fried fish. Fennel? Whatever, it was pretty good. It would also be bad manners to try to steal their cook, wouldn't it?

"I think I have chosen right in making this great valley my home," Qala said, hoping to turn the conversation away from matchmaking. "It is not yet overcrowded. Lots of room for me! It is a beautiful coun-tryside, and the weather remains mild despite it being midwinter. You know all this, of course — you live here!"

Lady Belema smiled warmly. Qala was making a good impression on her, it seemed. "You are upriver from us? Is that correct?"

"The old Damros estate," said her husband. "A few leagues further up Chas and on the other side."

"I own some on this side too," Qala informed him, "but the manor house and most of the estate is across the river. The land there is wilder and more lawless, and therefor cheaper!"

"Most true," agreed Hurrum. "But more dangerous. You must retain some men who know arms."

Qala had certainly intended to do just that. "I thank you for the advice, Hurrum," she answered, hoping to come off as rather innocent and demure. "Is it truly dangerous about here?"

"Weren't there reports of unknown men about?" asked Lady Belema.

The thegn nodded. "Strangers passing by. Boats on the river, too."

"No crocodiles, I hope," Qala muttered so only Corad might hear her.

He spoke, but not of reptiles nor of strange men. "Qala plans to purchase a boat for travel on the river. You should give her a tour of your boathouse, father."

"Most gladly. First thing tomorrow, before we feast, eh?" He looked up as Lovi entered. "Ah, dessert!"

The cook set a large pastry before them, and cut it open to expose the fruit inside. "Peach pie," stated Hurrum. "I had never heard of placing fruit within a pastry crust before Lovi came to us. Now it is my favorite!"

Qala found herself of a sudden choked with emotion. "I — I haven't had this since I was a little girl." Such memories it brought! And no, not all of them good but the former pirate felt homesick as she had not for many a year.

She ate the treat without haste, not speaking, and fearing a tear might come to her eye.

Maybe she should rethink stealing Lovi from Sarowhem, she told herself as she returned to her room, Domi going before her with an oil lamp. The thegn and his wife apparently had rooms on the first floor and she was not sure where Corad had disappeared. They had talked some time of inconsequential matters before she had excused herself. It was not so late but already quite dark out on this, the eve of the Yule.

She was also not sure she cared to sit in a chair while she ate. It was the Muram way to recline while dining, at least where Qala had grown up. Though she would as soon use a cushion on the floor, it would be best to buy some chairs and a tall table when she furnished her manor house.

Guests would undoubtedly expect them.

6.

"You Sharshites make so much of this day! Being Muram, I can now enjoy a second new year celebration at the proper time, the spring equinox. I do not mind feasting twice one bit, and I hope to be in my own villa by then."

It seemed that much of Thegn Hurrum's household would join them in this Yule feast. The hall was filled with their families, lining long tables.

"Then I must visit and feast with you there," chuckled Corad. He glanced toward the barely noticeable swell of her belly. "You wouldn't — no, of course not. Too soon."

"I would think closer to mid-summer. Depending on when exactly this happened to me."

"Father gave you the tour this morning? You can sit over there." The nobleman pointed to a seat near — but not at — the thegn's table.

"He did."

Hurrum had knocked on her door early that morning. Qala had, of course, already been up for some time and had devoured a breakfast Domi had brought. She was considering sending the girl back for a second one. "We had a religious ceremony to attend last evening," explained the thegn. "That is where Corad went, helping the priest set things up."

"Oh. I am sure my people have some sort of ceremonies too." She shrugged. "I couldn't tell you what they are."

"I'm not sure I can either. I tend to sleep through them."

Thegn Hurrum was tall, balding, middle aged, seemingly a mild and even ineffectual specimen of the landed gentry, but Qala knew better. Hurrum was a noted fighting man and could have a temper. He was also a major factor in the politics of the region, a man willing to work with the Muram regime. That was one reason his son had sailed against her pirate kingdom with a Muram fleet.

He had given her a tour not only of his boathouse but also the stables, of which he seemed inordinately proud. As his daughter, he loved horses and anything to do with them. But Qala could see those stables were old and become a bit shabby. As had all Sarowhem, if one stopped and looked at the place.

"My son-in-law stole one of my little boats when Marana kidnapped him." He laughed and Qala laughed with him. Both knew the thegn's daughter had been behind that escapade, though Hurrum swore to have Saj's blood at the time. "His friend Xit helped. Have you heard aught of him, Qala?"

"Not since I left Azer," she answered. It was the truth.

"His disappearance was strange," said the nobleman. "Some claimed he turned into the monstrous crocodile that was seen in Chas. Others said it ate him, or that a sea-serpent did." He shook his head.

"He *was* a wizard." That he was apparently also a god she did not intend to mention.

"Yes. Anyway, we never saw him again. Saj had to find a new second to stand with him at his wedding. Corad."

"Oh? I had not heard this."

"Corad has become your friend." The Sharshite seemed to muse on this thought for a moment. "As was Marana. So I shall be too, though I suspect you are not quite who you claim."

"Are any of us?" she had asked. She had lunched alone in her room after that, and napped as would a Sharshite, before coming downstairs to this Yule feast, wearing the same green grown as before. Qala regretted not bringing another, but not too much.

There were stacks of roast meat and fowl and puddings made of things she could not name. "I have never feasted with Sharshites before!" she exclaimed. "There is so much!"

Qala found herself seated with Hurrum's bailiff and his family, and a visiting merchant. The two men spent most of the meal talking of trade while the woman fussed at their numerous children. Qala knew little of children, having seen almost none for more than half her life. So the

Mur ignored them and ate. Then she ate more. She was hungry a lot lately, wasn't she? Maybe there was a ravenous little crocodile inside her. She was both amused and slightly frightened by that notion.

Those children looked like small hungry animals, didn't they? One little girl stared at her and told her mother, in a rather loud voice, "She has funny eyes."

"Hush, dear. That's not polite." The woman gave her an apologetic look. But Qala did have funny eyes, she knew. Muram eyes. She decided to smile.

"Looks like the priest is about to get up and blather for a while," the bailiff's wife whispered hoarsely. "I'm gonna scoot out of here with the kids before he starts up." Her husband nodded and looked as if he wished he could do the same.

Qala turned her head toward the table where the thegn and his family sat. Yes, there was a white-robed man, his beard long and streaked with gray, speaking into Hurrum's ear. "What god does that priest serve?" she asked.

"Jov, officially," answered the bailiff. "But he'll be wishing the blessings of Belore on us today."

"The sun god, right?" Qala had seen a great variety of gods in her lifetime and had never bothered to sort them out.

"Yep. Some of the common folk around here still honor Kamat, the old Ildin god of light, at this time of year. Used to be lot of Ildin living here and some of 'em married Sharshites."

The ancient deity Orgum would have been invoked where Qala had been born, and probably among the Mura here as well. Orgum was not a good sort of god and she felt it better not to mention him.

The priest's blessing — or whatever it was — proved short. It was also in Sharshic so Qala had no idea what the man said.

After that came drinking, from which the Muram woman excused herself. Too much wine would be good for neither her nor the life within her. Before slipping away to her bedchamber — Marana's bedchamber — she sought out Corad and spoke to him.

"It was good to share this feast with your family," Qala said. "I must be friendly with my neighbors and we have a further bond in your sister, my dear Marana. I am not sure what the thegn and the lady, your mother, know of that! But they were gracious hosts and I think maybe I grew on them."

"They approve of you, I believe. Father is happy to see someone taking residence at your estate again." He chuckled. "I understand he is procuring a boat for you."

"Yes, he promised to find me a little vessel so I can sail up and down Chas and visit Sarowhem frequently!"

"You will always be welcome, my lady Qala."

"But I shall not wear out my welcome. A day more maybe and then back to my new home." She sighed. "Back to the task of taking control of my estate and all the rest of it. And somewhere in there, I shall have to give birth! Pray to what gods or goddesses you know, my friend, that it goes well. I do not know if any would listen to an old pirate."

7.

The new ferryman seemed competent enough, Qala thought, and was not inclined to cheat anyone. Her power as a leader of pirates had been based on honesty and fairness above all else. Qala must have men she could trust in her service, men who would not cheat for a few extra pennies in their pouch. This ferry served primarily to carry farmers and their produce across the river. Her own prosperity here depended upon it doing so fairly.

Her villa she could see from across Chas. She could see, too, that it was in great disrepair, having been abandoned for many years. The lands about it were tilled by tenant farmers, their shacks scattered in disorder through the fields. All this she must change. In time. For a few days more, she decided, she would rest in this village and only cross over to take stock of her manor, as now she did.

Yes, she must have a name for it! Something in Sharshic, so it seemed to fit. So *she* seemed to fit. It would not do to call too much attention to her origin in the kingdoms across the sea. She must ask some of the locals about the proper words; Qala knew she might never learn much of the language herself.

And why bother, after all? Muram had become the common speech of trade throughout the empire. Qala stepped onto the ferry, leading Jacef. "Wait until the accustomed time to cross," she ordered the man at the sweeps. "A regular schedule is more important than my personal convenience." A pair of laborers joined them, and a girl with a cow. None were inclined to address their mistress, nor to speak at all. The ferryman pushed away from shore and paddled them, not hurrying, toward the far side of Chas. The river was still rather wide here and did not move too quickly. There must be a flood season. In the spring? She would have to ask about that.

Mist clung along the banks. The morning was still, and cold. The air felt hard. Qala grew inattentive, staring out over the water, her reverie ending only when the craft bumped unexpectedly against a dock. She led her horse onto land, murmuring a word of thanks to the ferryman.

Also unexpected was the young curly-headed fellow who now stood before her. "There she is," he cried out. "Thief!"

"Here, man, none of that," spoke one of the laborers.

He yanked a dirk from its sheath. Qala had her own dagger in her hand at once, ready to do battle, and it was most likely she would have come out the victor. Though one never knows, does one?

But the two workmen had already grabbed the boy's arms and his blade clattered onto the stone pathway. "You're the Damros lad, aren't ye?" asked one.

"Ranwif," said the girl with the cow. She shook her head. "You should be ashamed of yourself, threatenin' this nice lady. And her so small!"

He seemed properly abashed but Qala suspected malice remained in this young man. "What is this about?"

"His family used to own this estate," offered the ferryman, who had joined them.

"Aye," agreed one of the men. "It was confiscated by, er, your people years ago when they was caught conspirin' with the Pretender."

By 'her people,' he meant the Mura. Her heritage was always going to be something of an issue. Qala looked her youthful would-be as-sailant over. He probably lost more than the family estate, she thought. The family, too — Muram justice would surely have meant executions.

Indeed, the boy was fortunate he hadn't ended up on a cross or, at least, in the slave market.

"They weren't conspiring. It was all made up," he blurted.

"I wouldn't be surprised," was Qala's even response. "These things happen and they happen too often." All five looked at her in surprise. Not the cow; she was busy with a patch of not-too-withered grass she had found. "I'm not empire-born, you understand," she continued. "Just the wife of an honest merchant from across the sea. I've seen plen-ty of injustice on this side of the water." And plenty on the other side, but there was no need to mention that!

"Now I am only a widow hoping to live here in peace and raise the child I am carrying." All eyes immediately went to her stomach; if the people here hadn't known she was pregnant before, they would surely spread the word now. "I mean no harm to you, Master Ranwif, but all my savings went to purchase this home for myself." She sniffled, oh so slightly. "And my family."

One might become a pirate queen in many ways but one did not remain in power without knowing how to manipulate people. "Come along to the manor," she said. "If you know the place, maybe you could help me with it." Qala hesitated for a moment, not quite sure if she should say what she said next. "Know that you will always be welcome in your ancestral home." It seemed a likely way to win good will. Word of her magnanimity was sure to spread with that of her pregnancy. And it might even win this boy over, though she had her doubts.

It was better than having to knife him, anyway.

8.

Within a fortnight, Qala had moved into her villa, though she suspected the rooms she occupied were meant as servants' quarters. It would take time to make the main hall livable. More important to get the barns and stables fixed!

That main hall was filled with trash — there had been squatters — and cobwebs. At times, Qala felt sure the spiders were watching her from their webs in corner and rafter. Wondering when she might evict them, maybe! She laughed at that conceit but the feeling of being spied upon remained.

Ranwif proved surprisingly ignorant of the running of an estate. That disappointed Qala; the Mur had hoped he might be able to serve her as a bailiff of sorts. An unofficial bailiff, as one would not ask a lad of noble birth, no matter how far fallen, to take such a position. And he sometimes remained surly. So would I if another had taken over my home, she told herself.

Instead, she had given him an aristocrat's job in that home, that of bodyguard. Ranwif was modestly adept with weapons and, if nothing else, he provided someone with whom she could exercise her own skills. Qala did wonder where and when the boy received his training but did not pry. At least not directly.

Nor did he ask Qala of her capable handling of weapons, though it was obvious he wondered. Inevitably, Ranwif's abilities improved under her tutelage. So went the Month of the Crow — as the Mura count the passing of days — and came the Month of the Rabbit. Two boats also came up the Chas, and Corad with them.

"Father did not need to use all the funds you put at his disposal," said the nobleman, and waved an arm toward the small vessel he and a quartet of rowers had towed upriver. "It's a neat little craft, isn't it?"

Qala had to admit that it was not bad at all. Not a boat she would take into the open water of the sea, but suitable enough to sail Chas. "Small enough to handle easily on your own," he went on.

"Have you had her under sail?" she asked.

"How could I deliver her untested? She handles well." Corad grinned. "By my standards."

Qala nodded. Her standards would be higher, but the little sailboat seemed serviceable. "I thank you and the thegn," she said. "I fear I am too busy for even a little voyage right now. Are you staying?" She looked over his small crew of rowers. "Your men need a meal and night's rest.

"Ranwif," she called, without awaiting an answer, "will you escort these men across the river? Tell the innkeeper to feed them."

Young Ranwif looked unhappy about the request but did her bidding. "He wanted to remain here with the grownups," observed Corad. "That's the Damros boy, isn't it?"

"It is. Come along to my ramshackle house, Corad. I have not decided on a name for it yet. Or is it the estate that has the name?"

"Both. He is the last of his family, you know." The two strolled toward the manor house, in no hurry, across an unkempt brown sward.

"I did not," replied Qala. "I have not spoken to him of it. The rest were executed?"

"Some would say so. Others would say murdered. Ranwif was very young and out playing in the fields when it happened. I think one of the peasant families sheltered him after that."

Ranwif has been reared by more than just peasants, thought Qala, but she asked, "Does he have a noble title?"

"None that the empire recognizes." Corad left it at that. If he was surprised when Qala led him into the servant's wing, the Sharshite did not show it. "You're making progress."

"But I've no idea how to run a farm. I need a bailiff or steward or whatever to help me." Qala smirked. "Perhaps I should sail down to Sarowhem and offer some jobs."

"As long as you keep away from Lovi," responded Corad. "We near the Feast of Awakening. You could join us."

29

"Half way between the solstice and equinox, right? I should probably be with the people here." She corrected herself. "My people."

"Sensible. It is also our celebration of love, you know. The boys will be getting frisky."

Qala snickered. "Not just the boys, my friend." Her mind, for some reason, wandered to the girl Domi. There was someone she could hire away from Lord Hurrum. "Are you attached to some young lady yet? Where are those damned servants? I wanted to offer you wine."

"Not yet. There are various women of noble birth being mentioned to me, none of whom I have ever seen." Corad watched a seemingly distracted Qala disappear into the next room, to return with a jug and goblets. As she poured, he told her, "Word of your pregnancy has reached Admiral Murgom. His mistress, too." He cocked his head at her. "I think she is rather jealous of you."

"Had she any brains she would know better." Qala had briefly enjoyed the company of the woman — and the woman herself — during her time in Azer. A soft and sentimental girl, the sort she might become fond of but could not respect.

"In time it might make it all the way to his wife in Muradon. The consensus is that she won't care."

"I much suspect that when the child is born everyone will realize it isn't Murgom's." Qala sat down, facing her guest across a newly-fashioned pine table. It still carried a strong scent of resin. "That is why I spoke of my poor dead husband as being a trader from the southern isles."

"But you are not certain."

Qala shook her head. "No, not completely." Both sat in silence a moment, sipping from their cups. "You and your men can stay here tonight," the Muram woman eventually said. "I have enough rooms in decent repair now. I can even feed you, if I can find the servants."

"I thank you, my lady. I was only a boy the last time I slept in this house." He looked about. "My father brought me. Even then there were rumors of — treason, so we never returned."

"Some see your father as the traitor, don't they?"

"He is practical."

"I always approve of that. I think," said Qala, "I shall sail down to Sarowhem sometime before the new year, um, that is before the equinox, and visit. There will far too much to do here after that for any travel."

"Then we shall expect you, my lady."

9.

Qala did celebrate the Feast of Awakening with 'her' people. She had come to think of them as such, more and more. The pirates she had once commanded had never been hers in quite the same manner; their loyalty would last only as long as business was good.

Would business be good here? It did not actually need to be, as far as Qala was concerned. She could live in this old manor house on the money she had put away and let the peasants fend for themselves. But that would swiftly lead to boredom and boredom was deadly to someone like her. Better to take the helm again and steer this estate by whatever winds might blow.

"There have been strange men about," Ranwif reported to her. "None in town but they've been seen lurking along the road and in fields where they shouldn't be."

"How many?"

"Well, there's where it gets odd, my lady." She had told the boy to address her as Qala, but he seemed unwilling. Embarrassed, even. "There have been different reports. Some have seen what seem to be common ruffians — never more than three together. Then there are the others." He sounded rather perplexed by these. "There is mention of a small dark man, usually alone, though some said a woman accompanied him."

This brought Qala to attention as little more might. Could it be Xit returned to his man-form, to her world? When it came down to it, she rather hoped not. He was amusing and he was brave but he was a man — of sorts — and she needed none of those about right now. Nor any crocodiles, should he decide to visit in that form. It was confusing, was it not?

"Well, keep watch, my boy. I need to depend on you to run things here for a few days while I visit downriver." The old farmhands would actually keep the place going but it didn't hurt to tell Ranwif he was in charge. Someone might even pay attention to him if an emergency arose.

"You will sail?" Was there a wistful tone in the lad's voice?

"Yes, the maiden voyage. Hmm, I should name my little boat, shouldn't I?" She could not help laughing when the appropriate name came to her. "It is the *Marana*, of course!"

Ranwif did not get the jest; that was probably just as well. "Would you like to learn to sail, Ranwif?" she asked him. "It would be a useful skill."

He nodded and smiled broadly. "I would, my lady."

"But not for a while, I think," she continued. "There is going to be much to do and I, ah, may not be quite up to some of it. You understand?"

"Yes, Lady Qala! You can depend on me to take care of things."

The boy had become downright devoted, hadn't he? "I'll leave, um, the day after tomorrow. And I'll be back when I'll be back."

Qala did find herself on the river two days later and the *Marana* did handle pretty well, she had to admit, as she steered it down Chas. The flow of the wide stream was really enough to carry her along, and the sail could be used primarily to steer. Upriver, she would have to put more effort into working the wind.

Little lay upon the left bank; at places, forest grew down to the water's edge, with dark pools of shadow beneath the overhanging trees. There were shacks hidden further back in those woods, Qala had been told, the abodes of squatters and outlaws, runaway slaves. Much wild country was to the south, all the way down to the Lesser Sea.

To the right was mostly farmland but there, too, rose patches of forest. This was still something of a frontier, unlike the long-settled valley of the Indor to the north. It was as though the Chas created a sort of border between civilized lands and the wilderness. But Qala's estate was on the wilderness side of the river!

She reached Sarowhem by boat sooner than she might have managed on horseback. With a favorable wind, that might even prove true of the return journey. Qala did not care; she enjoyed being able to sail again. If only she could sail on forever, never worrying about anything again, all the cares and despairs of life. The Muram woman steered her craft, with all the expertise gained in a life at sea, to the Sarowhem dock, casually tossing a line around a post and making it fast. No one was on the docks, nor in the boathouse. Hurrum should keep a better watch here — a pirate just might land on his property one of these days!

Oh, here came somebody. Maybe there was a watch. Qala scanned the buildings around her. There were several vantage points up high where one might keep an eye on the river, but she could not pick out a watchman.

A pair of the thegn's men at arms were hurrying toward her. "It's the Lady Qala," spoke one. "We wasn't expectin' you, ma'am."

"Didn't Lord Corad say she might pop in?" asked the other. "And here she is! Welcome, m'lady. We, um — yes, we'll escort you to the hall, if that's alright with you."

"That would be fine, gentlemen. Could one of you bring my bag?" The two practically fought over which would have the honor.

A few minutes later she was sipping hot cider in Lady Belema's chambers. "Both my men are out," the lady of Sarowhem explained. "Lots to do with spring rushing toward us."

"So I understand," said Qala. "I know far too little of managing a farm."

"You would be surprised at how ignorant Hurrum is," the lady confided. "He really leaves the day to day running to our bailiff and spends most of his time with the horses."

"I suppose I need a bailiff myself."

"There are several knowledgeable young men about who could be interested in the position," said Belema. "Knowledgeable young women, too, for that matter. I'll mention it to my husband." She thought on that for only a second or two before saying, "No, I'll mention it to

Corad."

Yes, Corad was the man to whom she should speak, not only of hiring but also of those strangers Ranwif had reported. "I thank you, Belema," said Qala. "Am I keeping you from siesta?"

"Oh, I don't nap as a rule, especially not in this cooler weather. I retire to these rooms to rest and read until everyone is up and about again." The noblewoman nodded toward papers spread across a small, nearby writing desk of dark wood. "Also, I use the time for correspondence. A letter from my daughter has finally arrived."

"The Lady Marana is well?"

"She is. She and Saj spent some time in Matanas — which they thought a quite horrible place — and were preparing to head on toward Lanlaz when she wrote. The girl thinks they will settle there."

"It is a horrid town," agreed Qala. "I've been there — one great slave market! Of Lanlaz, I know nothing." That she had brought slaves herself to that market need not be mentioned.

Belema let her eyes rest on her guest's face. "Marana asks of you, of course. Shall I tell her of your condition?"

Qala felt slightly absurd discussing the matter. Whose concern was it but her own? "There is no reason you should not," she replied. "Perhaps she will have similar news soon."

"I do hope so." Belema smiled slyly. "That was a deft turning of the subject away from you, my friend." She spoke no more of it, for which Qala was thankful.

10.

"Do you like it here at Sarowhem?" she asked Domi.

The young woman had been laying out and smoothing the clothes from Qala's travel bag. The reply was surprisingly matter-of-fact. "Not much, m'lady. I used to be Lady Marana's personal attendant and that was good. I liked the lady. Bein' here by myself is no good."

She turned back to her work, hiding her face, but Qala thought she detected a sob. There was probably more to the girl's unhappiness. A man, maybe — well, make that a boy. "I could use a personal maid myself. Would you consider coming to my house?"

Domi turned, thoroughly surprised by the offer. "I — I don't know, Lady Qala!"

"Think on it. I'll speak to the Lady Belema, if you are willing." What had led her to make such an offer? The connection of this girl to Marana? Or had a bit of lust played a part? She actually did need a knowledgeable female attendant. The farm girls at her estate were hopeless.

The girl stood a moment, her eyes toward the open window. "Why not, m'lady?" A shy smile spread across her freckled face. "Why not?"

It was not Belema to whom she spoke later that afternoon, but Corad, returned from riding about the estate, 'keeping an eye on things' as he explained. "No one would object," the nobleman told her, but added, "You should know she is a natural daughter of Hurrum."

Qala could see that at once; in fact, she was surprised she hadn't noticed it before. Domi looked more like her half-brother than she did Marana, but not tall as were her siblings.

"My father would be glad to see her well situated. Mother, too, for that matter."

"Is her mother about the place?" If she were still Hurrum's mistress, it might lead to some awkwardness.

"Long since married. You met her at the Yule Feast — the bailiff's wife."

Qala had to laugh. "I hope her many bratty brothers and sisters don't come to visit!"

"Including this one?" asked Corad, winking.

"Always welcome, sir, bratty or no," she told him. Then Qala thought to ask, "Does the girl, ah, know?"

"I would assume so. I've never spoken to her of it."

"Then neither shall I. You'll approach your parents about all this?" That did seem best to Qala.

"I shall, and mention your desire to find a bailiff too. But remember that our cook remains off limits!"

"I commit to nothing when it comes to Lovi," she warned. "I shall head right back tomorrow and sail no more, I think, nor travel at all for a while. Domi can come up when she will."

They entered the private mural-walled dining area where the thegn and his wife waited. A slight man taking dictation from Hurrum, scribbling on a slate, was dismissed with a nod as the pair seated themselves.

"Accounts, Father?" queried Hurrum.

"Yes. We can discuss those later. Welcome, Lady Qala, on your return to our home."

Qala had heard the talk, even in Azer — Hurrum spent too much and was in chronic debt. She had also heard hopes that the more frugal and businesslike Corad might straighten things out now that he had returned to Sarowhem.

"I am pleased to accept your hospitality once more, sir," she replied, keeping it formal.

A thin soup was set before them by a boy of the kitchens. By now, Qala had learned that Sharshites tended to eat more heavily at midday than in the evening. She sniffed at the broth. Duck?

"I hear you have had reports of strangers," said Hurrum, after somewhat lowering the level in his bowl. "They haven't caused any trouble, have they?"

"Not so far," Qala replied. "It might mean nothing. Vagrants passing through."

"Possibly," agreed the thegn, and finished his soup. It was followed by broiled fish. Fish seemed to figure large on the menus of Sarowhem and, being on the river, that made sense. Some sort of mashed vegetable accompanied it, quite unrecognizable to Qala. Maybe turnip? No, milder. She didn't like it.

Hurrum again began a conversation. "It was good of you to take the Damros boy on," he said. "As a man at arms?"

Qala smiled. "Boy at arms would be more like it. Though I'll admit, he is not entirely useless with weapons."

"He would not have learned that from the peasants of your estate," said Corad.

"Didn't he have relatives somewhere he went to for a time?" asked Belema.

"He did," Hurrum said. "This is while you were gone, my boy. Some rumors say he spent time at the court of the Pretender."

"Best not spread those rumors," warned Corad. "They could get him executed — and any who might be connected to him."

Qala did not like either of those possibilities. "I should have more men at arms, shouldn't I?" she asked the thegn. "One half-trained boy seems inadequate."

The nobleman shrugged. "A few men who know their business can be useful for keeping order. If there is serious trouble, you will need to depend on your farmers and laborers to do some fighting. Best to get them organized."

Peasants as warriors? The idea sounded preposterous to Qala, who had spent her life around professional fighting men. "I suppose I could set Ranwif to do something with them." They might just follow the boy from old loyalties to his family. That presented other dangers, maybe. "But I think I had better take on a few veteran men at arms too."

"An excellent idea," agreed Corad. "What's the next course?"

11.

"There will be days the ferry can't operate but the flood is almost never too high to get a boat across," said the innkeeper. He and Qala looked upon the swollen stream. "The snows are melting in the mountains where Chas rises."

All this was new to the former pirate, who had never before dwelt by a river of any sort. She had found this innkeeper the most knowledgeable man in her little domain, both of what happened here and up and down the river. Qala made certain to sit and talk with him from time to time.

"Then Lord Corad will need to stable his horse here," she said.

"That would be sensible, my lady," the man agreed. "I understand your people make a big deal of tomorrow."

"It is the Muram New Year. Don't you celebrate the day somehow?"

"Oh, aye, we're not likely to forget Spring Feast. Some folks say it is sacred to Rema, the earth goddess."

"The belief of my people is not so different, though our goddess has another name." It was not necessarily Qala's own belief. She peered down the riverside road, the dirt pathway turned golden by the noon sun and sapphire-dappled by the shadows of the trees lining both sides. Those were leafing out now and many that would bear fruit were yet in flower. How the air had been filled with their scent this past fortnight! "I think I see him coming. Or someone."

Two mounts gradually took form in the shimmering distance. "He has brought Domi," she said to herself, but out loud. Qala was surprised by how much that pleased her.

"Domi, my lady?"

"My new girl. Attendant. Girl attendant."

"Ah." The innkeeper looked toward the approaching riders. "I'll pop inside and fix some lunch for all of you. Ho, Tom," he called to his stable boy, "two horses coming. Take good care of them!"

I am so swollen up now, Qala thought. *I must look quite hideous.*

And it will get worse! She resolved to hide from everyone for the next three months.

The groom stepped past her to take charge of the horses, as the travelers from Sarowhem dismounted. Domi attempted to lift down an unwieldy bag. "I'll take care of that, miss," said Tom. "Just leave it to me."

All her possessions, thought Qala, thrown into a sack. What might be important to the girl? What would she carry into a new life? "No need," spoke Corad, taking charge of both bag and half-sister. "I'll carry it on in."

Tom gave the nobleman an abbreviated bow and led the horses away, but not before letting his eyes linger on young Domi for a moment or two. Qala knew there would be a lot of young men giving her such looks here. Aye, older men too.

"I welcome you both," she said. "Are you staying for, um, Spring Feast, Corad?" Qala had almost referred to it as the Day of the New Year. There was no point in using Muram names here — even if it always would be the New Year celebration for her.

"I would be honored to be your guest, Lady Qala. I need to escape Sarowhem for a day or two."

Domi was gazing across the river. "Is that your manor, m'lady?"

"It is. I have chosen to name it Melawhem," she said, and turned to Corad. "I have been told that means Sailor's House."

The trio entered the small common room of the inn. "I think," said Corad, "I would translate the name as Seafarer's House rather than Sailor's House. It is a subtle difference, I know, dear Qala, but I think an important one. Either way, it is a good name, one that you might consider adopting as a family name. Melas, that would be." He looked to Domi, hesitating at the doorway. "Here girl, sit with us. You're not in our father's house anymore." He looked as if he immediately regretted the slip of saying 'our,' but Domi seemed not to notice it.

But she did, of course, Qala told herself. "Yes, Domi. Today you are guest, not servant." There would have to be a working out of how familiar the girl could be with her, and when. "But I shall put you to work, never fear!"

"Yes, Lady Qala."

The innkeeper brought bread and dried apples and tankards of sour beer. "I shall need to lean on you some," Qala continued, "over the next season."

"After, too," observed Corad. "You'll need a nurse." He looked fully at Domi and stated, "I expect you to take good care of the Lady of Melawhem."

12.

"This is the main hall," Qala told her companion. "Someday we will get it cleaned up and useful." It was still cobwebbed and dank, but no longer strewn with trash.

Domi surveyed the room. "It is a good space, m'lady. The hall at Sarowhem is too big and impractical."

Qala recognized the truth to that. She wondered if Domi had learned much of running an estate from her step-father. Surely some of the bailiff's knowledge had passed to her. Of a sudden, a movement in a shadowed corner caught her eye. A woman? No, there was nothing there when she peered again but she was sure she had glimpsed a dark woman standing in the gloom.

What could make her imagine such things? "Let's get back to the boys," she said. They had left Corad chatting with Ranwif while Qala had given her new maid a tour.

The pair was still sitting in the little room where Qala took most of her meals and conducted most of her business. Domi and Ranwif must be about the same age, she decided, though the girl seemed the more mature. She might be two or three years younger than Marana, her half-sister.

"We have been speaking of the unknown men your people have spotted," said Corad. Qala sat and motioned her new attendant to take the chair beside her. "A few days ago, I myself came on Lovi conversing with a stranger at the kitchen door. He said he was an old shipmate." Corad shook his head. "The man should not have been inside our walls without permission."

"Muram?"

"Yes. I sent him on his way. I might also have dismissed Lovi right there were he not so good a cook."

"He could have come upriver and found a new position quite readily," Qala said, with a laugh. She turned to young Ranwif and spoke more seriously, "Some said the men seen here looked Muram, didn't they?"

"They did, Lady Qala, but people imagine things."

They did. Qala reminded herself she did not believe in ghosts and tried to put her vision in the hall out of her mind. "We shall have a celebration tomorrow," she announced. "for the entire estate. Outdoors, if the weather remains good."

"You certainly couldn't fit them all in here," came Corad's dry observation.

"Can you feed so many?" wondered Domi.

"An excellent question, my girl, and a practical one. The peasants will, of course, bring their own food."

Ranwif said, "That is what they have done these past twelve years when no lord resided here." He bluntly told Qala, "If you are to be the mistress of this manor, you must act the role, my lady."

She looked to Corad's face. He said nothing but she could see he agreed. "Very well. You will continue to make sure I learn such lessons, Ranwif."

To Domi, she said, "I suspect you will have things to tell me, too. Never fear to say them. Ah, is our supper ready?" A middle-aged woman with patched and stained apron tied about her ample girth had entered.

"It is, m'lady. All four of ye?" She eyed the newcomer Domi with mild suspicion.

"Indeed yes, Fee. Mistress Domi will take supper with me most nights from now on." When Fee had left, Qala spoke in a low voice to her new attendant. "She should address you as mistress, as should the other household servants. You rank above all of them." She considered Ranwif. "Except the boy. You two must be equals. My right hand and my left!"

The young man did not look particularly happy about that. Good, thought Qala. He needs to remember he is not master here. Supper came, a thick, hearty stew and coarse bread — very much country fare.

Despite her jests about Lovi, a sophisticated cook was far down Qala's list of priorities.

Domi had not expected to be put in charge of the household so. She's handling it well, thought Qala. Or maybe she is just dazed! In fact, Qala had not fully decided to make such a move until that moment. But it was done now and she would see how it played out.

"It seems my parents may be marrying me off soon," Lord Corad was saying. "A niece of Gawif, of all people!"

"The noble who was to marry your sister?" she asked. "That seems an odd choice now. Wasn't he found to be involved in treason?"

"That he was. But the family remains wealthy and powerful and decidedly influential. Even the empire would not attempt to take all of them down."

"Ah. It is settled?"

"Still in negotiation. I've not even laid eyes on the girl. But," he continued, "it is rumored that Lord Gawif intended to marry her to the Pretender."

"Who is this Pretender? Saj and Marana mentioned him, and your father as well." Qala noticed that Ranwif was paying close attention to their exchange but attempting not to show it.

"A scion of the old royal family of Sharsh who now claims the kingship. He has no real power and hides out in a keep in the wild lands to the south, but those who hate Muradon may at least claim to follow him. Flawum is the name."

"Marana seemed to be a bit fond of him. She told me little, though."

"She thought the old boy rather silly and felt guilty of taking advantage of him to steal the Earth Stone. In and of himself he is harmless. It is what he represents that is dangerous." Corad became deadly serious, leaning forward and stating, "And keep in mind, Lady Qala, you lie not far from the borders of those lands where he still exerts some authority. If war ever came, you might be in its path."

13.

Qala was in the barns early and ordered a couple steers butchered for the feast later in the day. It was not a big thing, after all, and it would show her tenants that she had thought of them.

"What of a lamb or two as well, m'lady?" asked one of the farmhands. "That's sort of expected at Spring Feast." Qala found herself rather disliking the idea, having seen those lambs born not long ago, but told him to go ahead. "No more than two," she stated, her voice firm. She could not be queasy about such things if she was to run an estate.

"Too late to pit roast 'em whole," said another man. "We'll have to cut 'em up."

Qala did not stay for any of that, though she thought perhaps she should. This was her business now and she should know all of it. She could make the excuse that she had guests to attend.

The actual feasting began around noon and Qala was glad to see her tenants and employees handle the whole affair without needing her input. Thanks did come to her for the meat, and many wishes for the blessings of Rema, and thanks that there was a noble again in the manor house. That she was not a noble and dwelt in the servants' quarters was beside the point, Qala recognized.

There were games on the lawns of freshly-sprung green grass, and dancing to bagpipe and whistle. Maids and young men alike donned crowns of leaf and flower and, not unexpectedly, slipped away from the crowd from time to time.

Also not unexpectedly, much attention was paid to Domi. Qala could not help feel slightly jealous of that, but there was much to divert her from such thoughts. And she was no longer suffering the nausea that had afflicted her when first she came to Melawhem, though she tired more quickly than she liked. The former Pirate Queen was a person who greatly hated being at less than her best.

It was all she had, much of her life, her own prowess, her ability to best what the world sent against her. Now it had sent a little crocodile and it was laying her low! Still she had dreams where she truly did give birth to a reptile. What defense had one against dreams?

For the first time, she was acting the role of lady of the manor in earnest, seated at a high table — albeit a trestle set up in a field — and acknowledging her people. It was not so unlike being a queen of corsairs, was it? At least she need fear no assassination attempts here! Corad sat at her right, her guest of honor; it would not be proper for Domi to take such a position so she had been exiled to a nearby table, where the young men swarmed about her.

As for Ranwif, Qala was not sure where he was. The boy took his duties as guardian of her realm rather seriously, so he was no doubt off checking on one thing or another.

She could not bring herself to partake of the roasted lamb. With a baby within her, how could Qala eat these children of the fields? But the aroma of the seared meat awoke memories, memories of when she was nearly a baby herself. For a poor family in the Muram kingdoms, mutton was the height of luxury, the meat one could afford only on the most special of occasions, when one fowl or another simply would not do. We ate a lot of pigeon, didn't we? she asked herself. It had been ages since she had tasted pigeon. Maybe Lovi was knowledgeable in its preparation. She would have to ask.

Many had slipped away, mostly to nap. Some napped right there, spreading blankets or mats on the grass. Corad looked half-asleep, sipping at some tawny wine. She had ordered several amphorae before first journeying to her estate, but had left them mostly sealed. What was that over there? A knot of men approached.

Ah, an half-dozen sturdy farmhands, and Ranwif at their head. They had their hands on — three men, it was, poorly clothed and looking scoundrels. The vagrants that had been reported? Hmm, they looked rather like seamen, from the cut of their ragged costumes, the very way they walked. They could have stepped off one of the ships she had commanded.

And maybe they did. "Madame," began young Ranwif, "we caught these vagabonds digging up the fields." One of the farm laborers held up a spade in evidence. She could see two more in other hands. "Why, we do not know."

"It's not the first time," complained a man. "They've been leaving holes all over."

"Just 'bout every time we plant somethin'!" claimed another. "We've been right peeved 'bout it."

Corad had stood and was looking them over. "Searching for some-thing?" he conjectured.

"That's my guess, sir," stated Ranwif. He seemed rather proud of ap-prehending them. With good reason, thought Qala. The boy did well.

"Bring them to my quarters," she ordered. "We shall deal with them there."

14.

"You remain outside the door and guard it. The Lord Corad and I shall question these men."

Ranwif very much wanted to object, she could tell, but did as ordered. The men were disarmed, after all, and he would be right outside. The door shut and they faced the trio in Qala's chamber.

She looked them over. They *were* pirates, of course. Two appeared more or less Muram, the one of them a good sized fellow missing an eye, the other small and a bit misshapen. The third was quite black, but otherwise near as average as a man might be.

"So what were you doing here with these?" asked Qala, holding up one of the spades. The men looked guiltily at one another.

"We was searchin' for yer treasure," blurted the little bandy-legged one. By his appearance and accent, he was empire-born, perhaps in Muradon, perhaps in some port city of Arolin or Sharsh. "We know ye has it here somewheres!"

"Quiet, Sorg," hissed the bigger Mur.

"I know you," said Qala. "You were mate on one of the galleys." She sought a name and found it. "Augun."

He maintained a truculent silence, so she continued. "What treasure I have, lads, is safely in banks in Azer and Indabas and other cities whose names you need not know. You were wasting your time."

"But the man Lovi, he say you bring big wagon here," said the third man.

"Lovi will be in serious trouble when I return to Sarowhem," remarked Corad.

"You — how are you called?" asked Qala.

"Babo, my lady."

"A man of the southern isles, are you not?" A few such had always been among her pirate minions. Surely this was the black man some of the peasants had spied. It was silly of her to think it might have been Xit.

"I am, worshipful lady," he replied.

"So maybe your treasure ain't right here," spoke Augun, "but you can lay your hands on it. What if we was to tell this lord here all we know of you?"

Both she and Corad broke into laughter.

The Sharshite nobleman informed them, "It is too late for that, my boys. You are the ones who would be swinging if you attempted it." He let his eyes move slowly from one to the other. "I have the authority to string you up right here and now." *He is actually considering it,* thought Qala. She should use that to her advantage.

"I assume you are the one to come up with this ridiculous idea," she said to Augun. "How did you find me?"

Augun seemed uncomfortable, looking to his mates from the corner of his eye, before he cleared his throat, and began. "You see, Qala — should we still name you Qala?"

"Make it Lady Qala," she said. Qala had been enough of a title in and of itself when she ruled over pirates. Here, the name meant nothing.

"Lady Qala. Well, y'see, we kinda deserted right after you did. Things was all a mess back at the base, everyone fighting to be the new leader, so we took a boat and headed out." Little Sorg nodded a vigorous agreement. "When we sailed into Azer, there was all kinda talk about a woman we knew was you, so upstream we came!"

"Then we recognized old Lovi and learned somethin' of the lay of things here," added Sorg. "He didn't mean no harm, sir," he told Corad.

"True," agreed Augun. "Just being friendly to old mates." He shrugged. "And we figgered there must be treasure so we started, um, scouting."

"We sorry 'bout the holes," Babo added.

"You actually have the authority to hang these men?" Qala asked Corad.

"My father is chief magistrate for all this region. I would be recognized as his deputy. But," the nobleman told her, "as the governor of this estate, you could order them executed yourself. In theory." Corad chuckled. "No one would question it, anyway."

"I would never hang a pirate. It would be unbecoming for one who used to practice that trade." She noted the relief on the faces of the three. "Beheading would be my choice."

Augun gulped. "It is the custom," he admitted.

"But you have committed no great crime here. Elsewhere means nothing to me." I could be hung many times over for crimes elsewhere, she told herself. "I have made a new start here and you lads could too." She glanced at her companion. "Lord Corad permitting."

"As you will, my lady," said he.

"I need a few men at arms to keep an eye on things around here. You never know when strangers might start digging holes or something of the sort." She looked at each former pirate in turn. "Would you take service with me, as of old?"

"I will," Babo immediately responded.

"It sounds good," admitted Augun, and Sorg nodded his agreeement.

"Very well. Now, remember, that boy who brought you in is in charge. You follow his orders." They might not have liked that but none objected.

"And remember I shall have my eye on you," warned Lord Corad, "and a gibbet at the ready."

15.

Corad had crossed the river before dark, saying he would spend the night in the inn and ride for home at dawn. Qala had to admit she was glad he did not stay. She felt tired, too tired to even think.

"Go on on to bed, Domi," she told her maid. "I'll sit a while maybe."

The girl seemed uncertain. "Are you sure you'll be alright, Lady Qala? I can sit with you."

That would be nice. "If you wish," said Qala. Both were silent for a minute or so. "Tell me of yourself," said the Mur.

"I think you would have much more interestin' things to tell, m'lady," came the response.

"Yes, but I've already heard all my stories!" The girl giggled.

"I'm just an ordinary servin' girl at a country estate," said Domi. "Oldest of a big family. You know my dad."

"Both of them." Qala regretted it almost at once. Why was her tongue misbehaving?

"Oh, you know that — I guess you would. That's what got me the position of bein' Lady Marana's maid, I suppose." She looked up at her employer. "But we liked each other, as sisters should."

"That is good. Do you like horses too?"

Domi now laughed outright. "I did not inherit that family trait, m'lady!"

"Then you take after your mother? Will you tell me of her, Domi?"

"She came to Sarowhem when young to take service and, well, things followed. One might think Hurrum took advantage of a naïve servant girl but my mother bragged that she seduced him. Not to me, of course, but I've heard the stories! Who is to say which is true?"

"Perhaps both."

"Perhaps so, m'lady. It does take two, after all." She became silent. Thinking of the former lover she had left behind was Qala's guess. "I believe I *will* go to my bed, Lady Qala, with your leave." The girl rose.

"Certainly, Domi. Sleep well."

Qala sat, staring into the shadows beyond her single candle. The small fire had been banked for the night, embers glowing on the tile hearth. It would not be needed at all soon, not for warmth.

The shadows seemed to swirl, a mist of night, of cobweb and distance, and a small, very dark woman stepped out of their depths "I am Mawa," she announced. "It is time we spoke."

Had she not known Xido, her little Xit, Qala would have thought this dream or hallucination. But she had learned the gods were real — some of them, at any rate. "Are you the one who has been watching me?" she asked.

"You could tell?" Mawa seemed amused rather than surprised. "Yes, I or my servants have been keeping an eye on you." Her black eyes went to Qala's rounded abdomen. "And on what you carry within you."

The woman — she might be a goddess but she was certainly a woman as well — took Domi's vacated chair. A rather nice-looking woman, too, Qala decided, slender and supple. She wore only a skirt of some sort, woven of a silvery-gray thread. "I will be aunt to your child," she said. "Yes, I am sister to Xido and, no, I do not know where he is. Swimming some ocean, somewhere, is likely, being a crocodile and nothing more."

Mawa sighed. "Such mindlessness is tempting to those who are as we, doomed to immortality."

"Do you — ah, are you a, ah, crocodile too?"

The goddess' laugh seemed to mock all the universe, as had Xit's. "No, Qala. I become a very different creature. I am Mawa the Spider."

So perhaps the spiders in the hall *had* been watching her? Qala wasn't sure she wanted to know. "You are like him. Some." Now that she had looked on Mawa for a while, she saw that she also shared some of the Crocodile's ugliness.

"I suppose I am. I am half-sister to Xido; he has a twin brother but he is quite different. You would do well to fear him." Mawa fixed her dark glittering eyes on Qala's. "To fear all of us, maybe. We are not trustworthy at all."

"Yet you have been watching over me."

"I have, when I can, for the sake of my brother Xido. Others may watch when I can not but you are unlikely to notice them; I was sur-prised when you managed to glimpse me yesterday." Her eyes went again to Qala's belly. "What is within you may have had something to do with that."

"Will my child be like you?" To be mother to a god was not Qala's desire. A normal child would do fine.

"Who can say? Demigods are a mixed bunch. Know that we will be watching and, if need be, protecting during your pregnancy, but I shall not show myself again. No need to draw attention!" Mawa rose and disappeared into the shadows.

Qala could not help notice how nice she looked from behind.

Part II.
THE HATCHLING

16.

The Feast of Flowers passed and Midsummer after it. How much longer must Qala puff up like some homely toad? Since the visit of Mawa she no longer had any doubts as to her unborn child's paternity. Surely the birth would be soon!

That it would come before the next local feast day, Qala was certain. The Feast of Plenty or something of that sort they named it, and it fell in the Month of the Grasshopper by Muram reckoning, halfway between summer solstice and autumn equinox.

But would the offspring of a god — or of a crocodile — follow the schedule of a human child? Xit had claimed to be truly a man when he took that form. So he had told Saj and Marana, though he had neglected to inform Qala herself of his godhood. She had thought him only an odd, ugly little man, a moderately skilled wizard yet a most excellent lover.

And so vital! That was what attracted her to Xido, wasn't it? But it was not enough. How could a man ever truly understand her, even a man-god such as he?

The storms of summer came frequently, rolling in across the valley of the Chas. It would be a good year, she was told, a plentiful harvest. Already the hard pears were ripening, some to become the peasants' homemade wine, many to end up as feed for the livestock. Baskets-full were dumped into the pens of the swine, to their apparent delight. "The peaches will be a bit longer," she was told. Qala's knowledge of these things held great gaps, but Domi was there to fill them. More so now, when she was not as able to get out and see things for herself.

Too, the girl was teaching her some of the Sharshic language. It might prove useful after all to know what her people here were saying to each other. It remained the daily language of many. Qala knew she was making but a start on learning it.

It was unfortunate that Domi and Ranwif did not get along very well. One was forever stepping on the other's toes, meddling in what each considered his or her private domain. Vying for her attention, they were — for her love, in a sense. Intervening was becoming a tiresome chore.

Tiresome also was the loneliness she felt. Visitors were few; Corad was off somewhere on business for his family through most of the season. The rumors of an impending marriage for the nobleman had become more solid. Vasema was the name of the girl and she was, indeed, niece to the dead Gawif, as well as being attractively wealthy. Qala knew nothing more of the woman.

Yet another storm threatened, darkness rising along the southern horizon, when she first felt the contractions. Qala turned to Domi, who sat embroidering — what an odd skill, thought the onetime pirate — and announced as casually as she could that her child seemed to be on the way. "You'd best fetch the midwife, my girl." Thunder shook the roof above them, dust from the open rafters sifting down into the room. "Before it pours," she added.

Domi hurried out into the gloom while Qala rose to go to her own bed. Her water broke before she made it. Who will clean up this mess? she wondered. I should have thought of such things. The wind howled louder and in Qala's heart, for the first time in a very long time, came a twinge of fear. This was a situation she could not control. She felt as hopeless as when she had been a child, homeless on uncaring streets.

The door banged. A small, crooked woman, enveloped in a gray cloak and hood, rasped, "I am here m'lady." Was this the midwife? She didn't remember her being so slight. It didn't matter; Qala was happy to see her.

Now where was Domi? She let the woman guide her to her bed. "Out of these clothes, mistress," spoke the midwife and removed her garments in a business-like fashion. "I think 'twill be an easy birth, even with you bein' so small."

"I hope so," gasped Qala. "Should I pray to some goddess or another?" She meant that as jest but feared her voice did not convey it.

"Well," replied the woman, throwing back her hood, "it would be unseemly to ask you to pray to me, despite childbirth being one of my specialties."

"Mawa?"

"Yes. Best I be on hand, I thought, instead of your village midwife. Your girl became quite bewildered when she went looking for her and wandered about in the rain a bit. That I thought best, too."

Playing with shadows like her brother? Qala's face displayed her disapproval but she said only, "I hope she comes to no harm."

"Domi will be quite upset, I am sure, but her soaking shouldn't hurt her. She'll be back in a minute or two. Here, drink." Mawa held a tumbler of cool water to her lips.

A distraught Domi did burst into the room shortly after, to stand staring at the two. "It is alright, deary," spoke the goddess. "I'm here to take care of the lady."

"I — don't think I know you," said the girl, peering at the woman by Qala's side. Why was it so hard to make out her features? She rubbed her eyes but it didn't help.

"Don't stand there dawdling," ordered Qala. "Get into some dry clothes and then help the midwife. Do whatever she tells you!"

The confused Domi obeyed. Outside, the thunder rumbled all the louder and the trees swayed in the storm.

17.

It may be true that Qala cursed the gods as she gave birth and the god Xido in particular, but Mawa took no offense at this.

"There," said the dark-haired goddess, "that wasn't so hard." Qala cursed again, as only a pirate can. The Muram woman had little knowledge of birth so had no way of knowing whether hers had been easy or no. She could only give thanks to the gods' mercy that it had not taken over long and her boy was in her arms before the rise of the sun.

It was into clear skies that sun rose, the storm passed. "We will need to find you a wet-nurse," decided Mawa. "I can see that." She turned to the bemused Domi who had assisted her through the night. "You could find us one." She smiled. "And spread the news of the Lady Qala's son!"

Domi hurried off to do just that. "Do you remember what happened through the night?" whispered Mawa. "Besides popping out your heir, I mean!"

"There were others here, weren't there? Domi didn't seem to see them." Mawa nodded and Qala went on. "I thought I glimpsed a great hulking form. I feared he was going to harm the little one."

"He might have if he could." Mawa rethought that. "Or he might have intended to kidnap him. One can't be sure what goes on in Budo's mind." She giggled, which Qala thought rather inappropriate to the subject. "What passes for a mind in Budo," added Mawa the Spider. "He is Xido's brother. They hate each other."

"There was another."

"That would be my own twin brother, Lenco. Between the two of us, Budo wasn't going to get to you."

Qala gave a weary nod. "I'm not even going to ask what he might turn into."

Mawa laughed. "That, perhaps, is wise. And now I must turn into shadow and let the lovely Domi be your nursemaid. Farewell, my Qala, and farewell to you, little nephew." She backed into a darkened corner and disappeared.

Domi and not one, but two, women who might serve as wet-nurse returned to find their mistress asleep with her infant son in her arms. "He is so dark!" whispered one.

"His father was a trader from the southern isles," the other reminded her. "Here, I'll give him a feeding." Both took the newborn into a corner to fuss over him. Qala roused and looked about a moment in panic before spying them.

"He shall be named Zedos," she announced to the room, "in honor of his father." Qala had thought about this at some length over the previous months and had chosen a good Sharshite-sounding name. She meant to become much of a Sharshite as she could for the sake of this boy. Her son should not feel like an alien in the land of his birth.

She held out her arms and the child was brought to her. "He will be tall and handsome, m'lady!" one woman assured her. Qala much doubted this. Small and ugly was most likely, and not looking the least like a man of Sharsh. But, as his father, the little lad was already surprisingly well endowed. Were Xido's brothers so? she wondered.

"The midwife should not have left you alone!" stated Domi, obviously upset. "I still am not quite sure who she was, either."

"That is not something you need worry about, Domi. All has turned out well. Is Ranwif out there?" She strongly suspected the boy was just outside the door. The girl nodded. "Send him in, then. I have something private to tell him."

All understood this as an order to leave. The young Sharshite entered and stood for a moment gazing at the boy. More curiosity than aught else, Qala told herself. "I have learned that, um, enemies of my late husband might mean our son harm," she told him. "I want you to be on guard for any threats. Especially a big ugly fellow who might be lurking."

"Yes, my lady! You may depend on me." He cocked his head at the little one. "Some rumors said a Muram admiral was the father. I can see that isn't so."

"No, he was a valiant sea captain from the south. I must have conceived just before the pirates took our ship and slew him." She sniffled loudly. "Now I only hope to raise our son in peace here on this estate."

"Oh, my lady!" The boy looked stricken. Hadn't he lost his family in such a fashion? She almost regretted having laid it on so thick.

"No matter, Ranwif. That is all the past now. We both have lives to live, don't we?"

"We do indeed, Lady Qala. Should I summon a priest here for the naming ceremony?"

She had no idea what that entailed. "We'll speak of that later," Qala told him. She could depend on Domi to explain it to her. "Do send the others back in now, will you?"

The boy would need to be officially recorded as a Muram citizen, this she knew. They might be part of the Sharshite landed gentry but his status as a Patrician must also be recognized. Her agent in Indabas should be written, and the birth entered in the Viceroy's records.

And if a bribe were necessary, she was willing to pay it.

"Bring me some breakfast," was her greeting to Domi when the girl reentered her room. "I worked hard for it last night! And do get someone in here to clean this place up."

18.

"The lad would be a Pirate Prince, wouldn't he?" asked Augun, as he stood on the dock beside his mistress. "What with you being our queen and all."

Qala knew it was the man's attempt at a joke. Maybe it was even amusing. "Never say that around here," she warned. "It is best that no one put any of our names together with the word pirate."

"Oh, aye, m'lady. He's a prince none the less. A fine boy."

She regarded him from the corner of her eye. The ruffian had seen Xido at their base, hadn't he? He would know enough to be discreet about that. "Here they come," she said, though it was rather obvious.

The ferry pulled away from the far shore. One man, one horse — not counting the ferryman, of course. Lord Corad had journeyed alone. She found herself embracing him, which seemed quite odd. She had never been so demonstrative before. "Welcome, Corad," said she. "I have missed your visits."

He laughed easily. "I would think you had enough to keep you busy, Qala."

"Too much! Having you here gives me an excuse to avoid my duties." She glanced up at the tall Sharshite. "Not that I consider my son a duty."

"Two weeks it has been?" The two strolled toward her manor house, Augun leading the nobleman's steed.

"And a busy two weeks, I will tell you. One of those festival days came and went —"

Corad nodded. "The Feast of Plenty."

"Yes. It marks the beginning of the harvest season or something, doesn't it? There is plenty to harvest. I'm told it has been a good year but everyone could be lying to me!"

"Even with the cost of the repairs I think you will come out ahead this year."

"Oh, I know I will. I do not neglect my balance books. Domi is a great help there. She is so busy running the place she does not have time to be my maid!" Qala spread her arms in mock exasperation. "And when she is not working at that, she spends much time holding Zedos. More than I ever would be likely too."

Corad seemed uncertain how to respond to that admission. "It is not in me, my friend, I know this," continued Qala. "I love my son but I look forward to the day I can train him to use a sword."

The nobleman shifted the conversation. "It will be known everywhere now that Admiral Murgom is not the father."

Qala nodded, somewhat absently. "From his coloring — not to mention the timing — there should be no doubt that Xit is the father." She though it best not to mention Mawa's corroboration of this. "Fortunately, the boy does not look in the least like a crocodile."

"Fortunately, indeed," agreed Corad. "He must take after your imaginary deceased husband."

Qala snickered. "I do hope he does not have the ability to change into a crocodile like his sire. Or was Xit a crocodile who could turn into a man? Be that as it may, when my son asks of his father, I shall name Xido and say with truth that he went off to battle and never returned.

"Let us hope he never returns, anyway! Like your brother-in-law Saj, I think I prefer my gods on distant mountaintops. Not in my bed!"

They had entered the main hall. "Nearly ready," Qala announced. She had been hesitant about evicting the spiders but the place was thoroughly cleaned now. "There are repairs to be made yet. And furniture. You Sharshites don't like to sit on the floor."

"You should be able to hold your Yule celebration in here."

"And that will mark a year spent in my new home. More or less."

"An eventful year."

"As was the one before it. The truth is, Corad, too many of my years have been eventful! I want peace now." She looked over the empty room before going on. "And someone to share it with. Oh, my son, of course, and maybe that will be enough. Maybe."

"You are not one to settle for less than you think you deserve, my lady. This I know."

"Ah, but just what does an old pirate deserve?" Qala's laugh was mocking. "Marana promised that the goddess Esefa would send me love. But for now I have no eyes for even the most attractive girls here — though I do notice that they are attractive so maybe there is hope!"

Corad seemed hesitant but he said, "Domi?"

"I think not. But I admit I have have made no, ah, attempts. I do not want to spoil our friendship. But what of you, Corad? I hear you are betrothed!"

"Yes, the match has been made official. I still have yet to meet Lady Vasema, but am told she is young and not too bad to look upon."

"According to Marana's tale, this Vasema's uncle was a hideous and loathsome beast."

Corad laughed loudly at that. "Most considered Gawif a quite handsome man. That he was loathsome, however, I will not contest."

"Having dwelt among pirates, I know something of loathsome, my lord. Come, you must meet my little one." They left the hall by a side door, crossing a narrow lawn to Qala's apartments.

"Loathsome as he may have been," Corad continued, "his lands are still attractive. Some of those lands will come as a dowry."

Qala scowled. "A most distasteful custom, I think. Although the opposite is even worse, the groom paying a bride price as in some nations. Muram women are not bought and sold like slaves!" She considered this thought before going on. "Unless, of course, they *are* slaves. I was surprised to see so few of those here. I was also surprised to learn your people so thoroughly disapprove of slavery. It makes disciplining ones servants properly much more difficult. But when in Sharsh," she concluded, "do as the Sharshites."

19.

"The marriage is set for the solstice," said Corad. "Yule Feast at Sarowhem. I can get you invited if you wish." He would know she would have little desire to come but probably should as a neighboring landowner.

"More than a season yet," said Qala, making no commitment on the invitation. "Surely you will get a chance to meet the girl before then."

Corad took a quaff of his ale before answering. "I have visited the estate on occasion but never ran into the girl. Of course, Gawif governed there then, not his sister. It is not all that far, over the hills."

The two were in Qala's private chamber, the one that served as both dining room and office. Zedos slept nearby in a crib, newly carved of oak, as they partook of a late and light lunch. Cold fowl and bread, and freshly brewed ale from the innkeeper's crocks, they shared. The young people, Domi and Ranwif, had been dismissed. They might be napping; it didn't matter.

"Mother and I are going to go visit the family next month. I should meet her then."

The boy stirred and then let out a prodigious squall. Corad regarded the dark little face. "I think he is hungry. Do you —?"

Qala shook her head with some vigor. "I attempted it but I have already dried up. Zedos has two wet-nurses to take care of his needs." She picked the baby up, rather gingerly. "And we have cows and goats and such. But this lad is soaking. That I can do something about."

Corad backed away from the odoriferous undertaking. He had perhaps even less experience with the care of small children than his host.

"He certainly sounds like a member of the family," came a voice like the wine of sun-blessed southern vineyards, at once sweet and powerful. A lean dark man, not very tall, was stepping out of the shadows in the far end of the room.

Corad's hand instinctively went to the knife on his belt. "Xit?" He looked more closely. "No. But you are much like him."

Qala agreed. "You must be Mawa's brother."

He bowed to her. "Lenco, my Lady Qala, at your service." The ebony eyes gave her a frank and appraising up-and-down. "I can see why the Xit was also at your service!"

Mawa abruptly stepped out of — wherever, and stood beside him. "Lenco is terribly crude," she apologized. "Xido has all the manners in the family."

"And this," Qala explained to Corad, "is the Lady Mawa, aunt and midwife to little Zedos. I welcome you back to my home, my lady. May I present Lord Corad?"

A smile that seemed a little too knowing came to her face. "I have watched Corad more than once in this house. With pleasure."

"Now who is being crude?" complained Lenco. "I'm supposed to be a god of love so at least I have an excuse."

"A god of sex, dear brother. How many times do I have to tell you that?"

"I still say it's the same thing." He turned to the mortals in the room. "We've been arguing this for millennia."

"You are gods," said Corad, perhaps not quite believing.

"We are?" laughed Mawa.

"I think so," said her brother, "except when we are something else."

"True. We are somewhat human at the moment. It is necessary."

"And fun, sometimes," added Lenco. "Beats being a snake."

"If you are human then you are hungry," said Qala. "Come have some lunch." Xido had always had a considerable appetite — for all sorts of things. "If you can stand the smell."

"Barely notice it," claimed Lenco. He looked over the stripped child. "Yes, definite family resemblance."

Qala wrapped Zedos in new swaddling and returned him to the cradle. She knew her technique was, at best, haphazard but the boy's nurses could sort him out later. His uncle wore a long kilt, not unlike Mawa's skirt, but looser.

Both gods seemed quite willing to munch hard bread and swig ale. Both also looked something like Qala's onetime lover, the father of her son, Xido the Trickster, Xido the Crocodile. But, well, more handsome. They had the same lean, muscular bodies, the slight stature, the black skin and eyes. Were those human bodies a choice? It would impolite to ask that.

But she could ask other things of them. "You are brother and sister, right?"

"Of a birth," said Mawa.

"That is the way with our pantheon," explained Lenco. "Most of us are twins. Must have something to do with our original worshipers."

"They created you?" wondered Corad. "I have heard philosophers claim such things."

"We always existed, at least in potential," claimed Mawa.

"As do all things," added Lenco. "Some would argue we did not truly exist until men discovered us."

"And others wouldn't." Mawa laughed. "Another thing we've argued over for a very long time."

"Recognizing that it can't be answered. But returning to your original question, my lady, Mawa and I are twins. Xido and Budo are also twins and half-siblings to us."

"Different fathers," explained Mawa. "Mom took a lover somewhere along the line."

Lenco gave her a look from the corner of his eye but said nothing. Qala suspected maybe Mawa the Spider had her own share of lovers — and she knew enough of the habits of spiders for that to chill her. What sort of relatives did she have here?

"Anyway," spoke Mawa, "we have heard that Budo has become interested in his nephew again." She nodded toward Zedos, once again fast asleep. "His attention seemed to wander after his previous visit."

"You have to understand, Budo is not the brightest member of our family," spoke her brother.

"It would be simpler just to say he is the most stupid," came Mawa's comment. "You've always had a soft spot for the idiot."

"Budo is not entirely to blame for things," maintained Lenco. "Xido was forever playing tricks on him." He looked straight at Qala. "Your boyfriend can be exceedingly unpleasant at times."

Mawa had objections. "He's mellowed. We all have."

"But he is still a crocodile."

"And what are we? But we digress. Budo may come snooping around again and we have no idea what he may intend."

"Considering that it's Xido's boy," said Lenco, "probably nothing good, though it could be simple curiosity, I suppose. He's not really malicious, you understand, he just has a grudge and does stupid things sometimes."

"Does he look like you?" asked Corad.

Mawa glanced at her sibling before answering. "Some. He's taller and broader and uglier."

"You can tell he's Xido's brother if you look him in the face," added Lenco. For a while, he sipped ale and gazed at the sleeping boy. "He has power in him," he said at last. "That may be a part of this."

"I know," said his sister. "I could sense it even before he was born. Maybe he should come live with us."

Qala rose, alarmed. "Fear not, my lady," spoke Lenco the Snake. "I will not let my sister steal your child. His destiny lies in this world, not ours."

"You are probably right," sighed Mawa. She rose and disappeared into the shadows. Lenco gave a mocking grin, bowed, and followed her.

20.

Ranwif had something on his mind; that she could tell. "Qala," he began, his voice overly resolute. "I have been thinking about us."

Us? That did not sound so good. "Yes, Ranwif?"

"The year is winding down, most of the crops in, and — and it's time to think of other things. Of the future."

"Your future? Are you thinking of leaving me?" Why not? she thought. She couldn't expect the young fellow to hang around here forever.

"Our future, Qala. I am asking you to marry me." He had managed to say it, and seemed both pleased and apprehensive. "Think what a good arrangement it could be."

So she did think and decided he was right. "Yes, it might well be a good arrangement, a practical arrangement. It would put a further stamp of legitimacy on my ownership here and it would bring the estate back into your family."

"But I would be cheating you. I am growing old and am unlikely to bear another child. My boy, I am twice your age!"

Ranwif dismissed that argument. "Women a decade your elder give birth," he pointed out.

"And many are grandmothers by that time," countered Qala. "You know I would not love you. You deserve love, young man." To that she added, her voice firm, "So do I."

He deflated. "You love Domi." It was not quite an accusation; more like the recognition of an unwelcome fact.

"No, no, Ranwif. I like Domi and I like you. And I wish you would like each other! But —" But what? Did she have hopes there?

"You could find love elsewhere and still marry me. I wouldn't be jealous."

Qala actually found herself considering this. After all, if she married any man it would not be for love. It would be for the stability of her home, for the sake of her son. She looked again at Ranwif. No, not this boy. It truly would be unfair to him.

And to the girl he was bound to meet someday. That was the thing. He might love Qala or think he loved her but it would not last. "You are too young," she said. "But maybe you won't always be." Perhaps it was wrong to give him that sliver of hope but then maybe it was as much for her as for him. Who could see what needs the morrow might bring?

Ranwif left, therefor, dejected but not defeated. That was to the good and things would play out as they played out. Maybe she would find someone to love eventually; she was not feeling quite so disinterested now, with pregnancy and childbirth becoming a memory. She was feeling like Qala, the queen, again.

Corad would be off to visit his intended bride around now, on her family estates in the upper Indor valley. A sister of the late Lord Gawif held those estates; all the descendants of Gawif — who were surprisingly few, considering the man's reputation for lechery — had been stripped of any rights to them. Some had fled, fearing outlawry or slavery.

None of that concerned her, but the girl would be a neighbor and the wife of a friend. Maybe Corad was her best friend in this new life of hers. The man she had once enslaved — now there was a jest! If he had come to her with an offer like Ranwif's, she might just have taken it. That, of course, would never happen nor would they ever be lovers. Maybe that made their friendship safe for both of them.

There came a rap on the frame of her open door. It was Babo, holding up a piece of paper. "Message come, Lady Qala. It is important say man?"

"Come in," she told him, and held out her hand. "When did it arrive?"

"Only right now. Horseman in village he give me and ride away!"

It bore the seal of Thegn Hurrum. Whether the cramped script inside was from the nobleman's hand or a secretary's she did not know, but the message was the same. *The Lady Vasema has been kidnapped, possibly by followers of the Pretender. Corad is gathering men to go after her and may pass through your lands. Please give what assistance you can.* Ah, it was signed in a broader hand, *Hurrum*.

Qala did not know what help she could offer but her friend could count on her. She should call her men together and find out if anyone had seen anything — the Mur was well aware that travelers and smugglers bound for the southlands would often pass near or, sometimes, through her estate. If there were ever peace and legitimate trade she would be in a most excellent location.

Babo still stood there, awaiting instruction. "Go find Ranwif," she told him. "He was just here so it shouldn't be hard. Tell him to gather his men and come to the hall."

21.

Corad rode in the next morning with four equesters. "I want to travel quickly," he told Qala, as the men and horses were ferried across Chas in two trips. "There should be men at arms along in time under one of our captains."

"Can I help, Corad?" she asked. Qala rather wished she could saddle up Jacef and join him. No, she was as skilled with weapons as any man but her horsemanship was not so good. And she did have a baby son, after all, not that Domi and the nurses couldn't take perfectly good care of him!

"Feed us and send us on our way," he answered. "There's not much else."

Ranwif and the three former pirates — they had taken to referring to themselves as his 'crew' — approached. "Sir," said the youthful leader to Lord Corad. "I have been in the south. I might be able to guide you."

The nobleman's eyes immediately went to Qala. "It is acceptable to me. If the boy could be helpful, take him along."

"Get your horse and gear. We move on within the hour."

"I have a meal laid out in the hall," said Qala, as she led the men toward her manor. "Babo!" she called, "You remain as guard on the river crossing. Augun and Sorg with me."

"I sometimes forget you were a leader of men," mused Corad. "I do suspect, my dear Qala, you could do all this better than any of us."

"You needn't suspect," she answered. "It's the plain truth. So when did they steal this girl?"

"Before ever I arrived at her home. I still haven't set eyes on her!" He shrugged. "But we are betrothed so it is my duty to try to fetch her back. I almost wish she would stay kidnapped."

The hall held not only a meal for Corad's men but a number of farmhands who had conflicting stories of seeing mounted men passing through. The Sharshite nobleman listened with patience to their accounts. "I can't really make any sense of it," he admitted to Qala, once the men departed.

"Ranwif already heard their tales and thinks there might be something to them. You'd best trust him." She looked as if saying the next words left a bad taste. "But maybe not too far."

Corad nodded. "He remains friendly toward the Pretender, you think?"

"Not unfriendly, anyway. He should not be put in a position where he has to take sides. And —" Qala frowned. "He is a bit unhappy about things right now. I will not tell you why but I know that can lead men to do what they might not otherwise."

"Understood." A short time later, six men rode south along one of the dirt cart paths.

Qala watched them go and then turned to contemplate Augun and Sorg. "I suppose one of you should be in charge of our security while Ranwif is gone." Augun seemed the logical choice but she did not completely trust the man. Moreover, he was something of a bully. That was not a bad thing on a pirate galley; here, where he must deal with her community, it was a different matter.

"Sorg," she ordered, "go relieve Babo at the dock and send him to me. I'll be in my chambers. You patrol," she told Augun. "There may still be strangers about and I trust you to guard my property." She didn't, that much, but it would be good to give the one-eyed scoundrel some responsibility. Qala turned and headed for her apartments. Babo was the man to put in charge. He had more brains and, perhaps more importantly, was not Muram. It mustn't appear that she practiced favoritism toward her own people. Sharshite peasants would grumble about that.

She passed by her hall. Qala was tempted to think of it as 'the great hall,' as Hurrum's folk termed his. But it was not nearly as grand, so that might seem pretentious. She stepped in to find it empty, all evidence of visitors and a meal already cleared away. The mistress of

STEPHEN BROOKE

Melawhem chose to cut through the building rather than go back outside and around.

To a doorway in the shadowed arcade along the western wall she headed. A form moved, off to her left. A man? Yes, a rather large fellow. He stepped forward, almost seeming to coalesce from the darkness, and held up a broad hand.

"Do not fear, lady. I mean no harm." He looked quite a lot like Xido, she realized, if Xido were a head taller and had put on too much weight.

"You are Budo," she said.

A grin came to the god's decidedly ugly face. "Yes, lady. Budo the Boar I am!" He seemed pleased to be recognized.

"Call me Qala. We are family, after all."

"Family? Yes, family." He nodded vigorously. "But you were my brother's woman." Budo scowled at that thought.

"Long past. It was but a dalliance for both of us."

The big man-god squinted his eyes, suspicious of her statement. "Xido would not have given you a son if he didn't like you."

Qala sat down on a rough board bench pushed against the wall, and patted the place next to her. Budo took a seat without a word. "You don't care much for your brother, do you?"

He shook his head. "No, Qala. Xido isn't nice."

She had to laugh. "True, Budo. I would never use that word to describe him." Qala was surprised that Budo joined her laughter. "And he left me quite alone to bear and raise his child."

"I will help," stated her large companion. "You must watch out for Mawa and Lenco. They are not always nice either!"

Aha! There was always more than one side to a tale. "But you hate your brother. Why would I trust you?"

"Who would hate a baby? Not Budo! I could keep him safe in my cave and teach him, um, god things." He gave Qala an appraising look. "You could come too. Xido does have good taste in women!"

73

"I thank you, Lord Budo, but our life is here." Maybe Budo was being sincere or maybe he just wanted to show up his brother. How better than to steal his son and woman? "You are ever welcome to visit."

The look he gave here was both shy and eager. "Tonight?"

This oaf in her bed? Well, yes, he *was* a god and, yes, celibacy was becoming quite monotonous. "Maybe soon," Qala replied, and realized that was not unlike what she had told young Ranwif. "I have business to attend right now, and a son as well," she said, rising. "I hope he turns out as handsome as his Uncle Budo."

She left the tongue-tied god standing in the shadows and passed out the door.

22

"You are certain this is the shorter way?" asked Corad. Again — he remained mistrustful of both this boy's loyalties and knowledge.

"Absolutely, my lord. Most follow the main road without questioning its course, but it was laid out with wagon traffic in mind. On horse-back, we can take a straighter path."

Well, that made sense. He and his men continued to follow Ranwif down the narrow track. It seemed fairly certain Lady Vasema and her captors were on the road south. They had found the tracks, four or five horses it looked to be, and were told by local peasants of the passing of armed men with a lone woman.

Now if Ranwif's trail could get them ahead of the group! It led them, in time, to a spot where it crossed the main road. "No one has been through here," reported one of the men, scanning the dirt.

"Then we ride back a way and set up an ambush. Come," ordered Corad. The road seemed lightly traveled; after all, little trade passed through the disputed lands to the south, though some attempted this overland route to the coasts of the Lesser Sea, rather than taking to ships. Woodlands bordered it on either side, great oaks of the primeval forest.

But here and there would lie a field, a cottage. The peasantry here was not so secretive as those who dwelt further south. There, they built their homes, tilled their fields, in hidden clearings, avoiding the troops of both Pretender and Muradon, as well as roving outlaw bands. There was little authority to rein in the latter.

"This is as likely a spot as any," spoke Corad, signaling a halt. "Keep to the horses and get into cover. No, all on the same side so you may use your bows."

The six quickly concealed themselves. To Ranwif, their leader whis-pered, "Keep out of this unless you absolutely must, lad. It's not your fight, anyway." Corad had been surprised the boy even owned a sword when he had shown up with it strapped to his waist. Hadn't Qala mentioned something about training him?

No matter, here they came. Four? No, five, and one of them the girl Vasema, surely. She was hooded so he could not make out her features, nor even the color of her hair. He could trust his two archers not to shoot in her direction.

The men themselves seemed little more than lads. Armored well enough, however, with hoops of iron about their middles, infantry-fashion. All carried lances and short swords, and mismatched helms were on their heads. The last thought to pass through Corad's mind before he signaled and the bow strings twanged was that the fools were using the old-fashioned saddles with no stirrups. Some Sharshites refused to employ this Muram innovation — an innovation that had helped them conquer. Then he and his men charged forward, as one of the enemy tumbled from his seat.

Ranwif drew his sword but, as ordered, did not enter the fray, sitting a bit apart on his horse. A clash of blades, shouts, hooves pounding. Then it was over, four kidnappers on the ground, all of Corad's men unharmed, save for a few scratches and bruises.

And no sign of the captive. "She bolted, off that direction" said someone, pointing. "I don't blame her!"

"Natural thing to do when attacked," muttered another, as they sat their mounts and surveyed the bodies of their erstwhile opponents.

Ranwif lowered himself beside one of those bodies. "I know this man," he said. "He was a bastard of Lord Gawif." Ranwif remained squatting, staring at the calm, youthful face. "We played together as children."

Corad dismounted and placed an hand on the boy's shoulder. "Why don't you go search for the girl? We'll take care of burying them and meet you at that crossroads back there by dusk." Ranwif rose and nodded. As soon as he had ridden off, the nobleman instructed his retainers to toss the bodies into the ditch and throw some branches over them. "No sense wasting time here."

They searched the woods until near dark, finding no trace of tracks, and met up with Ranwif at the designated place. "We will camp here tonight," decided Lord Corad. "Tomorrow we search further."

"How long, my lord?" asked one of the equesters.

"If we find no sign whatsoever on the morrow, there would be no point in searching further through these woods. We would fall back to Lady Qala's and meet my men at arms." He shrugged. "If the girl has any sense at all, she rode toward the river." Lord Corad did not sound like he actually trusted Vasema to do so.

Nor was there any evidence she had the next day, though they searched up and down the road, and along paths that led away from it. She had vanished into the trees and there was naught to be done. Corad and his men started home with the rising sun.

23.

"This girl came riding up to the fences, very quick-like," reported Augun. "She wouldn't say who she was or what she was doing there so we brought her in." A pair of farm laborers stood behind the man at arms.

A runaway from somewhere was Qala's guess. That was of no concern to her. Sharshite — that was obvious — and moderately tall. Lean, even rather muscular. A girl who used her hands, maybe from some farm. Capable farmhands were always welcome if they were willing to work.

"What do we call you, young woman?"

"Sesa, my lady." Hmm, she didn't have a peasant accent. At least not one from around here.

"Very well, Sesa. If you would like a job, you can stay here. Otherwise, my men will return your horse and escort you from my property once you have rested." She addressed Augun. "Is it a decent mount?"

He only shrugged. The former pirate knew little of horses. One of those who accompanied him spoke up. "So-so, m'lady. She musta rode it hard. Looks nigh worn out."

"Then see to its stabling first, Sesa, and then come back here and we will speak. And get a meal into you." Her visitors filed out and Qala turned to Domi, sitting nearby and rocking Zedos's cradle back and forth. Domi was a pretty girl, wasn't she? Qala liked to just sit quietly and watch her do such things. Most likely she would never do more than watch.

"What do you think of our guest?" she asked.

"She is not a peasant," replied Domi. "Sesa is a made-up name, don't you think?"

Qala nodded. "That is why I asked what we should call her, not what her name was." The girl might be from some villa, a lady's maid as was Domi. "If she can read, she would be wasted doing farm chores. If she wants to stay at all."

"Do think she's runnin' from somethin'?" Domi rose from her place, and stretched.

"Or someone," said Qala. "I would suspect so. If Sesa thinks this is far enough away, she might choose to stay." She looked over her attendant — or maybe aide would be a better word these days. "Why do you persist in wearing shoes in this wonderful weather?" Qala went barefoot as much as possible, as she had in her days of piracy.

"Wonderful, my lady? Too hot for me!"

"It is never too hot," objected the Mur. "I would it stayed like this year 'round!"

Domi sat again and idly placed one hand on the cradle, rocking it slowly. "It must have been hot in the southern seas when you sailed with — with your husband." She looked at the sleeping Zedos. "I am sorry that he is not here to be with you and his son."

"So do things go, my girl. And you needn't absolutely believe all of my story about him." Domi gave her a look of surprise. "But, yes, it is hot on the steamy southern seas. Half my life I spent there." She paused, seeming to be lost in some thought or another. "But half I spent in the grim gray Muram cities across the Great Sea. That is why I would as soon never feel cold again."

For a time, they spoke no more. Domi went to her embroidery work, Qala to her account book. A rap came on the door, not too loud. Since the birth of Zedos, everyone on the estate had been warned not to make too much noise.

Domi let their visitor in. Again Qala looked her over; not impressive next to her maid, but Sesa seemed a healthy, even sturdy, girl. She had lank hair of a nondescript brown, pulled back tightly, a prominent nose. Deeply tanned, she was.

Darker than I am, thought Qala. I should spend more time in the sun.

"How old are you, Mistress Sesa?" she asked.

"Seven and ten, my lady," came the answer. Domi was scarce older.

"You can read and write?" was Qala's next question.

"Yes, my lady. Also ride and shoot the bow and track any beast through the woods."

Qala managed to maintain a passive expression, though interest and amusement both fought against it. Might she be some gamekeeper's daughter? "Those are useful accomplishments," she admitted, "though I know not whether we need them here. Do you think you might be willing to stay?"

"Perhaps, my lady." Sesa was not giving anything away either.

"Well then, sit down and have some lunch and we shall talk about it."

24.

Corad and his riders returned late the next day, Ranwif with them.

"Twenty of yer men are camped across the river, sir," Sorg informed him as he alit from his steed. "Awaitin' yer orders."

"I'll need them over here. Send word for them to come over." He noticed the man's hesitation. "What is it?"

"Well, beggin' yer pardon, m'lord, but I'd have to run that by Lady Qala first."

A moment of irritation came and went. "Of course. I've overstepped myself. Ranwif," he called, "will you run and ask your mistress if my men can cross?"

The young man, who had been subdued and spoken little since their battle, saluted the noble and set off. He found Babo loitering on a bench outside Qala's apartments, an empty mug at his side. "Captain Ranwif," the southerner greeted him, rising. "I stand guard here." He turned toward the door, hanging open on this day, still hot, almost too hot, though evening approached. "You go in."

Two women he expected; three he found. Some girl from one of the farm families? He ignored her for the moment. "Lady Qala, the Lord Corad wants to know if he can bring his men at arms over."

"Babo," she called, rather than replying, "do run down to the landing and tell them to ferry those soldiers over. Ranwif can keep an eye on things here."

"Yes, mistress." The man headed off toward the river.

"So," she said, turning back to Ranwif, "I take it you were not successful." Qala laughed when he looked puzzled. "Sesa," she spoke to the unknown girl, "how would I know this?"

"Lord Corad would not need his men had he found his lost bride," she answered. Ranwif thought the little smile she gave him contained a trace of mockery.

"Right, my girl. Poor Ranwif is undoubtedly worn out and not able to think right now." It sounded like Domi attempted to stifle a snicker.

He did not deign to look her direction.

"Then we should offer him a chair and refreshments, my lady?"

"Indeed. It is near supper time. Eat with us, Ranwif," invited Qala. Or perhaps she ordered it. Either way, he would be happy to sit down and fill his stomach.

"You post a guard at your door, my lady?" he asked, taking a seat.

"Certain occurrences have led me to be more cautious," she replied, sitting down beside him. "Not for my safety but for that of Zedos. Is there any wine left?" she asked no one in particular.

"Babo got the last of it," said Domi. "Why don't I go get another pitcher and bring our meal too? Come with me, Sesa." Sesa did follow her out the door but not before she and young Ranwif exchanged glances, only to swiftly look away from each other again.

"She wandered in," Qala told him. "I decided to take her on as my new maid, so Domi can concentrate more on helping run this place."

"Do you know anything of her, my lady?"

"More than you might think," came Qala's enigmatic reply, "and more than she realizes."

The girls returned with fried pork and griddle cakes and a large jug of ale. Ranwif found himself called upon to relate his recent adventure as he filled his stomach. He did not mind at all this audience of three somewhat attractive and attentive women — briefly four when Zedos's nurse came in. She was not so attractive but she did listen to him talk.

But he was starting to have trouble staying awake. It had been an exhausting ride south and back. At last Qala ordered him off to his bed and he was not too reluctant to go.

"You'll see more of him," Qala told Sesa. The look she gave the girl seemed innocent enough. Then she added, "Lord Corad too, undoubtedly. He's quite a handsome and charming man."

"He's *old*, isn't he?" asked Sesa.

"Not very," objected Domi, who seemed to feel obligated to defend her half-brother. "Only, um —" She tallied it up in her head. "Eight and twenty years."

Sesa laughed. "How would you know that? Are you sweet on the man yourself?"

"He is my brother," she blurted out. Domi had not intended to tell this, but she had been provoked, hadn't she? "Half-brother."

"Ooh." Sesa regarded the young woman she now worked beside, the woman who might be a friend, and said, "You will have to tell me more about him."

This did not surprise Qala at all.

25.

Benaro was an old friend, a friend of Ranwif's childhood. Practically his brother, for the man's family had taken him in after the loss of his own. He listened without comment to the tale of the journey south with Corad. At its end, however, he stated, "You need to be choosin' one side or the other."

"I prefer to be on my own side," Ranwif told the man. The pair sat on the front porch of the tenant farmer's modest cabin, several dogs of uncertain ancestry lolling nearby on the rough boards. "I hate the Mura, you know that, Benaro. But Qala has treated me well and I've no quarrel with her." That he had some hopes there, he did not say. They were vague hopes and would evaporate and reappear with some regularity.

"The Lord Corad is no friend. His father stood by while — while it happened."

Ranwif only nodded. Thegn Hurrum was not blameless in the murder of his parents, his sister, his entire household according to the accounts he had heard. Corad seemed a decent enough man but, no, he was not a friend. "Should I, then, serve the Pretender? He will never lead us against the Mura, my brother. I spent time in his court, remember, and came to know the fop."

"I call him the Ri of Sharsh, not the Pretender," came Benaro's vehement response. "Our true king."

Ranwif's words were equally emotion-filled. "Were he truly the leader of our people, my family would still live." Both sat a while in silence, sipping the young farmer's homemade wine. "I chose not to accompany Corad south this time. I suspect he will not find his intended bride."

"Lost, you reckon? Let me refill your cup there."

"Maybe. It's not our concern, in truth."

"You helped only to please your Mistress Qala," said Benaro. "I could see that." Benaro would never refer to the Muram woman as 'Lady Qala' and, strictly, he was correct in that. She had no noble title.

"That is probably so. She has a new maid, did you know?"

"Aye. Not too bad lookin' either but she seems kinda stuck-up. Domi's nicer — I was thinkin' of payin' her court."

Ranwif laughed. "Be my guest!" He drained his wooden cup and stood. "I need to be on my rounds. You have work too, I am certain."

"Nothin' that won't wait. I'll mostly putter in my own garden today." Benaro's smile was broad. "Or maybe go visit Mistress Domi."

It was true that there was not much that needed done in the fields on this day. Give it a couple weeks and everyone would be busy with one harvest or another. Ranwif walked a dirt path between two fields of ground nuts. Those were an important crop here — some of the country folk ate them but most served as feed for the livestock. Indeed, the bulk of what grew on Qala's estate was intended to fill that role.

And after the harvesting there would be butchering, as cool weather started to set in, and the salting and smoking of meat. Had anyone checked the smokehouses to make certain they were ready? Ah, that was no concern of his; he was neither owner nor bailiff here.

Yet Ranwif could not help thinking of the newly-renamed Melawhem as his. If only Qala — well, he doubted that would happen now. Perhaps Benaro was right about things. Perhaps he should return south and place his hope in Flawum, the Pretender, actually doing something someday.

One of the local boys he had been training as a sort of militia stood guard before Qala's rooms this morning. The lady had informed him that she did not intend to move from those rooms until spring returned. All the empty days of winter could be used to get the living quarters in the manor house readied. The quarters his family had once occupied.

Only Sesa was inside. No, that was wrong; Sesa and Zedos were inside. The girl looked rather harried. "Why couldn't your mistress give me work I know how to do?" she lamented. "I know nothing of babies!" The little one squalled in her arms as she jerkily rocked him.

"Here, give the lad to me," Ranwif said. "Has he been fed?" She willingly handed off the child to him.

"The nurse but left. And he is dry."

The young man felt. "Dry-ish. What troubles you, little master?" Ranwif, unlike this girl, knew a good bit about babies. Growing up among peasants had educated him well in such things. He put the boy across his shoulder and, not unexpectedly, Zedos burped loudly.

"Oh, he has made a mess of your tunic!" cried Sesa. Then she giggled. "Better yours than mine."

"You could bring me a rag, if you're not too busy," he told her. "Where is the Lady Qala this morning, anyway?"

The young lady wiped his garments somewhat clean, as she told him Qala and Domi had crossed the river to speak business. "Merchants of some sort," she said, "staying at the inn."

Buyers of farm produce, Ranwif suspected, perhaps hoping an inexperienced Qala would sell too soon for too little. They were likely to be surprised; indeed, they might well be fleeced themselves. The Mur knew how to deal.

Little Zedos spat up again. "That's likely to be all," he told Sesa, and placed the boy in his crib. The child fell asleep almost immediately. "So just what duties are you suited to, Mistress Sesa?" he asked.

"Something out of doors! I am more suited to minding a kennel of hounds than a child."

"And maybe riding after those hounds, as well? Our lady keeps no dogs. I suppose she never has, what with living on a ship and all."

"I would like to do that someday," said Sesa. "I mean sail on a ship. To — to anywhere!"

Ranwif understood. He had some similar dreams hidden away within himself. "Lady Qala has a little boat. She has promised to teach me how to sail it sometime but we have both been kept too busy."

"Having a baby must be a great inconvenience," allowed the girl. Ranwif was uncertain how serious she was being.

"Well, isn't that what women are supposed to do? Give their husbands children, not ride about in the woods."

"I can see you have learned little from Qala," sniffed Sesa. "Maybe when I reach her age I would consider taking time for a baby. And with any luck, the father would not be around!"

"I think perhaps he would not want to be." He at last gave up trying to maintain a straight face and in moment or two, Sesa was laughing as well. Ranwif thought he liked this girl quite a bit.

26.

Someone there in the darkness? Qala whispered, "Budo?"

"Budo?" came a laughing feminine voice. "You haven't been letting him into your bed, have you?"

"And why not?" The Muram woman sat up. "I might be tired of sleeping alone, Mawa."

The dark-eyed slender goddess came and perched on the edge of her bed. With the window shuttered against the night and any light of stars or moon, Qala could barely make out her form. "Ah, then it hasn't actually happened."

"No. But he wants it. That's why I thought it might be he."

"Well, Budo is every bit as, um, talented as his brothers. I knew he had spoken to you; I still have many little eyes about the place to keep watch."

"He warned me against you and Lenco."

"A warning to heed, my dear. I have told you before the gods are no more trustworthy than humans." She sat still for a moment. "I was tempted to steal away your little one to live with us. I suppose I still am."

Qala reached out and found Mawa's hand. "Have you no children?" she asked.

"So many I can not remember all their names, going back to the darkness before humans knew us and we were not sure what we were, ourselves. Some were monsters and some were heroes; some died as will mortals and others yet live with us, or have disappeared to find worlds of their own. Yet I too am often alone, Qala."

"You needn't be. We needn't be, at least tonight." She pulled Mawa toward her and found her willing to come.

Not unexpectedly, the goddess had vanished, come morn. This did not bother Qala, nor did she spend overmuch time thinking on what had happened. She found one of the wet-nurses tending to Zedos in her common chamber, which served as well as nursery for the boy. The girls must still be sleeping.

For now, those two shared the other room opening into this one, as had Domi since arriving. It must be a bit cramped, thought Qala. Or maybe they enjoyed having each other's company. Girls that age seemed to. At that age, herself, she had been learning her bloody trade, already a highly-skilled swordswoman. Aye, and falling in love with the woman of a pirate king.

She gazed for moment at the ring she wore still on her left hand, a ring with a small white diamond, given her by that woman she had loved and who had loved her. The jealous chieftain had slain her, taken her away forever, and Qala herself had slain him and taken his kingdom. It had not been enough to make up for what she had lost.

Qala did not know if anything ever would, but her infant son came closer than aught before. The door to the other room cracked open and someone peeked out — which girl, she was not sure. "She's already up," came a too-loud, hoarse whisper. A moment later, both showed themselves.

"We didn't bother you last night, did we, m'lady?" asked Domi. "We stayed up and talked for a very long time." She exchanged a conspiratorial look with her companion.

"Not at all. I noticed nothing." There had been other things to keep her attention. "Is one of you going to go get us some breakfast? And make sure there is fruit with it!"

"I shall, my lady," spoke Sesa, and scuttled out the door. Qala could see a light, misty rain was falling. There would be no harvesting today.

"And I'll fix your tea," spoke Domi. That was one of Qala's few indulgences, a habit of the southern isles she had picked up long ago. None here had even known what tea was when she arrived. She would allow herself this one luxury, procured by her agent in Azer and sent up to her now and again.

The girl busied herself with heating water. The fire was already blazing; the nurse must have taken care of that sometime earlier. "Will you stay for breakfast?" Qala asked the woman.

"No, m'lady, I'd best get back to my own family." The nurse rose and carried the baby to his mother. "Aarh, I am sore. The wee lad really clamps on!"

"Like a little crocodile," said Qala, taking her son.

"Indeed, Mistress Qala!" The woman nodded a farewell toward Domi and took her turn going out into the rain.

"That is some sort of private jest, is it not, my lady?" asked Domi. "About the crocodile, I mean. I've heard you say things such as that to my brother."

Qala came and took a stool by the fire. "It is a reference to the father of Zedos," she said. "That water should be hot enough. It needn't boil."

The girl added the tea leaves and set the pan to one side of the hearth, then turned a quizzical face toward her mistress. "His father was a crocodile?" Domi smiled, perhaps at the absurdity of her question.

"He was. Let me tell you the story. Hmm." Qala paused. "We'll wait for Sesa to come back. I would like you both to know it and its telling will fill a dreary morning."

27.

"There was simply no sign," Corad told her. Fully a fortnight had he and his men been gone. "I would like to remain here at Melawhem for a time longer, in case some word comes."

"With all your men? Not that it is a problem." But provisions would need to be made for them.

"I shall send most of them home, Qala. Keep my four equesters here, maybe, if it is not inconvenient."

"As long as you need, my friend." A hay wagon trundled by them, drawn by a pair of rusty-red oxen. "We are busy right now."

"It will be equally busy at my father's estate. If no news comes in the next few days, I shall head there myself." He seemed pleased with his plan, apparently just then having decided on it. "It is only half a day's ride to return, if need be, and that is not hurrying."

"I wonder if Domi would like to go back with you and visit. I've never thought to ask her anything of the sort and it *is* close." She stopped walking and turned toward the tall Sharshite noble. "By the way, I gave her the entire — well, almost entire — story of our adventures and who I am a few days ago. The new girl, too. They've become friends."

"New girl. I saw her, didn't I? Looked to be a skinny farm girl."

"Yes, before you headed south again. She has proven quite useful to me."

"Good, good. I hope you won't regret telling that tale." They were approaching her quarters. "Any more encounters with Xit's relatives?"

Qala only smiled. The sentry let them into the small apartment. A fire played upon the hearth, welcome in this cooler weather. Domi dandled the baby before it. "Don't get up," spoke Corad. Despite being half-siblings, there was a gap of age and station between them, he a lord and she a servant, and she afforded him the called-for deference. "Where's the other girl?"

"In the stables," came the answer. "She is almost as crazy about horses as the Lady Marana."

Qala laughed aloud at that. "If we gave her a sword, she could be one of your equesters, Corad."

Domi looked up at Lord Corad. "Wasn't that the station of Ranwif's father, sir?"

He knelt down beside the girl and held a finger out to the baby. Zedos regarded it with some gravity. "Under the Muram Empire, yes, that was the sole title he could claim." He looked up to Qala, who remained standing. "That is more or less noble, as you know, but not hereditary. Under the kings of Sharsh, he would have been styled the Mor, the head of an aristocratic family. That title is outlawed now, of course."

"So Ranwif is without any real standing, and without property." Qala thought on this a moment, before lowering herself to the floor, sitting cross-legged as she oft had, on ship, in port. If she accepted his proposal of marriage, that would change. Was she really considering it?

"I was thinking of offering him a place among my men," said Corad. "He could be elevated to equester in a year or two."

Domi shook her head. "He would have to swear loyalty to the empire. I don't think he would ever do that." She hesitated before going on. "I don't think he likes our father much, either." Then, quite changing the subject, she told Qala, "All the new account entries have been made. The books are over on the table."

"Thank you," said the Muram woman, rising again to her feet in one easy motion. "You've worked hard."

"Don't thank me. It was Sesa who did it all. She's way better at it."

"Maybe I *could* do without you for a while. Would you like to go visit at Sarowhem sometime, Domi?"

The girl did not even have to think about it. "No, Lady Qala. I've no reason to go there anymore. Unless it was as your maid."

Corad did not look the least surprised. He too rose and idly glanced at the ledger entries, penned in bold, looping figures. That tight and tidy hand on the previous page must be Domi's.

"Will you go find some quarters for Corad and his men?" She asked Domi. "Four of them. Hand me up my boy." The girl lifted her son to her and rose to wrap herself in a shawl and slip out.

Qala rocked the child in her arms. "I am getting better at this," she announced. "Aren't I, my little crocodile?"

Corad started, hesitated, then started again. "You needn't tell me, my lady, nor would I press you, but you said nothing of Xit's relatives when I asked. At least let me know if they have threatened you in any way."

"Threatened? No, yet I must consider them threats. Lenco I've not seen since he spoke to the both of us. Mawa, well, she has visited and we are friendly." Definitely friendly. She would not mention Budo. Qala did wonder why he had never come back.

"That is enough. I'd best get to the stable myself and see to all our mounts. Perhaps I'll run into your Susu."

Sesa, Qala corrected him, but not aloud.

28.

The scion of Sarowhem remained but two days before mounting up and heading home. "Expect my return," he told Qala. "I intend to ride back and forth until we learn something."

"You and your men are welcome always," she replied, even while tallying up the cost of feeding them in her head.

"Most likely I'll come alone. Farewell," said Corad, saluting her and turning his horse toward his destination. The equesters followed.

"There would be no reason for Lord Corad to bring men with him," she remarked to Ranwif as they walked to the ferry.

"Yes, my lady. Searching again would surely prove fruitless."

He knows, thought Qala, or at least suspects. They crossed Chas without further words. The harvest remained in full swing and there would be little else to think on for the next several days.

Yet she noticed that Ranwif often seemed to be around 'her' girls. Not favoring one over the other, necessarily, but he had not been so friendly when it was only Domi, his rival.

Domi and Sesa seemed to have become great friends. Perhaps that was to be expected, being of an age and better educated than the other young women about Melawhem. Could Domi and Sesa be involved? The thought had not crossed her mind before and if they were, of which should she be jealous? Oh, neither, of course. Let young people be young people and keep out of the way, whatever they might be up to.

To keep her mind off such things, the former queen of pirates decided to work in the fields herself. How better to learn? The sun would do her good, as well; too much time had been spent indoors this past year! It felt good to dig mindlessly in a field of ground nuts, turning the up-rooted plants over to dry in the autumn air.

It took her mind off the fact she was alone again, too. Mawa had not returned, nor any of Zedos's other supernatural relatives. How could gods maintain interest in what was going on in her little corner of a world that was not their own? Perhaps their disappearance meant, at least, that there was no threat to her boy. Knowing that was good enough.

She kept a sentry on her door, none the less.

When Qala did not work, she escaped in her little boat, sailing up and down the river. Not far either way; she had nowhere to go but much, at times, she wished to leave behind. Ranwif must receive his promised lessons someday, and Zedos, too, when he had enough years.

Work on the hall and manor house could progress one of these days. There was no hurry on that. Qala had picked out a suite on the lower floor for herself, first ascertaining that Ranwif's family had not dwelt in those particular rooms. No, she had been told by Fee the cook, who had served that family, those had been the apartments occupied by the bailiff and used for business. The family had lived upstairs.

Good, there would be less awkwardness then. The quarters she had chosen seemed more practical anyway. Qala wandered through those quarters, toward evening, thinking about nothing much — where a table might go, how close Domi's room should be to her own. And Sesa's — well, she didn't really expect her to remain here, did she?

The setting sun threw its light through one of the windows, a shimmering, golden light diffused by the dust-laden air. Something else shimmered, as if there were another source of illumination there in the room, a door opening to a world of light.

Through that door stepped a tall fair woman, clad in a long, sky-blue gown. A golden circlet bound golden hair. "I understand foreign gods have been hanging around here," she stated. Rather haughtily, Qala felt.

"I am rather foreign myself, my lady," she murmured.

The goddess looked her up and down. "This is true. You Mura confuse us since so many of you have taken to mixing us up with your own gods. Some days I am not even sure what my name is!"

Qala knew the truth of this. The Mura here had taken on the Sharshite pantheon in some degree and equated their own gods, the gods they brought with them across the sea, with those of Sharsh. That was not true in the old kingdoms where she had grown up. "You are the Lady Esefa, are you not?" It seemed a good guess.

Her visitor's face softened. "I am. Esefa, queen of the gods." Of the Sharshite gods, thought Qala. It would not be wise to say it aloud.

"By whatever names we are known," continued Esefa, "many prayers are addressed to us. I fear that we never hear the bulk of those prayers. Most of us are not omniscient, you know. But there is a girl down in Lorj who frequently mentions your name."

"Marana."

"Hmm, yes, that could be it. It does not matter. She keeps asking me to send you love." The goddess drew herself up in a self-important manner. "That is my great specialty!" She turned her deep violet-blue eyes toward the Muram woman. "You need a good man, do you?"

How to answer that? "A good woman might be preferable, my Lady Esefa."

"Oh!" Qala was surprised to see relief on the goddess' face. "That is always easier. Men are so difficult, you know."

"I do." She couldn't help smiling.

Esefa sat down on a packing crate. "My own Jov is a handful, I'll tell you! He is forever chasing after mortals of either gender. And pretty much anything else that will hold still long enough." She stopped of a sudden and scrutinized Qala. "You've had some experiences with our kind yourself, haven't you?"

"My little boy is the son of Xido."

"Xido? Oh — I, um, have met Xido." Her expression suggested she might have done more than meet him, or had at least wanted to. "That's why the Trickster's relatives have been popping in here, is it?"

"Yes, my lady. Mawa, for the main part." Qala sighed despite herself, but the self-absorbed goddess did not seem to notice.

"The Spider. I never liked her much. Well," she said, rising to her feet and considerable full height, "I'll see what I can do for you. Don't expect miracles, even if I am a goddess!" Esefa chuckled at her own joke. "I must come back and meet your little boy some time."

With that, she dissolved into sunlight. The room seemed suddenly quite dim and Qala realized dusk had fallen outside. She should hurry home herself to that little boy.

29.

When Corad returned he was, as promised, alone. "I'll stay out of your way," he told Qala, "and ride out to see if any news can be found or talk with travelers here at the inn. I have little hope now that the girl will ever be found."

"Outlaws, you think?" asked the innkeeper, hovering near the two.

"Or wild animals or thrown by her horse or any number of things. My father does hear of things that happen at the Pretender's court — not right away, you understand, but in time — and she is not there." The nobleman shook his head. "When cold weather comes we might as well put an end to the search."

"You never know," said Qala. "Some peasant family might have taken her in."

"Oh, I suppose so. But shouldn't we have heard of that? A woman of noble birth would surely stand out." He drained his cup and rose. "I might as well start. Will you cross with me, my lady?"

Qala had thought she might sail this morning but agreed to accompany her friend. "The Lady Vasema's parents are coming to Sarowhem," he informed her as he saddled his horse in the inn's stable. "It will be hard to tell them of all this."

"And you think there is no hope."

"None, Qala." He tightened the cinch and turned toward her. "I feel guilty admitting it but I am somewhat relieved that I need not marry this niece of Gawif. I believe I would rather take some girl of the countryside as wife."

"We have many from which to choose," teased Qala. "Shall I have them paraded before you?"

"Ha, I might yet ask it!" They parted company on the far side of Chas and the Mur began to walk toward her apartments. No, she decided, I am hungry. She changed course and angled toward the kitchens. These had now been moved into their old original location behind the hall, rather than the cramped shack that had been used when Qala first took possession of her estate. Mistress Fee now ruled over a pair of scullions and a large brick oven. It had taken some time to clean that and its chimney of the nests of rats and of swifts.

The food, however, was still country fare, filling but unsophisticated. Good enough for Qala but she might have noble guests here someday. It was to hoped, anyway, for her son must be accepted among the Sharshite landowners. As she sat eating a plate of eggs and bannock, Ranwif came and took a seat across the simple pine table.

"Lord Corad rode west," he reported. His face betrayed no thoughts on this fact.

"He'll find nothing," was Qala's only comment. "Aught else to report?"

"The hay is being cut in the low field," said Ranwif. "Sesa is keeping an eye on that."

She looked up from her meal. "You like Sesa, don't you?"

"Some. She's terribly stubborn and willful, and not really much to look at. Not that I care so much about that. But, well, Lady Qala, you know I can't let my thoughts go in that direction."

"And why is that?"

"Because she is Lady Vasema!" claimed the boy. "As I think you know, my lady."

"Yes, the girl is Lord Corad's bride-to-be, obviously, but she doesn't want anyone to know it. I intend to keep her secret and you will too." She laughed. "Don't give me that look of disapproval, young man!"

"But shouldn't the lord be informed?"

"If she does not want to be the Lady of Sarowhem, that is up to her and no one else." Qala was quite emphatic.

"Very well, my lady, I shall say nothing." Ranwif appeared discomfited by something; for a moment Qala thought he might speak further but he seemed to decide to hold his tongue.

Instead, he returned to his earlier point. "She is still a member of a powerful noble family. I would be a fool to aim so high." He gazed at his employer for a moment, and then spoke with candor. "I still have other hopes, as well."

"That remains unlikely, Ranwif. Yet I will not say never; one can not see the future." She had no desire for this boy. No, not really. But some - one who loved her and would remain with her — surely that was worth having.

He did not understand why she smiled then, but Qala was thinking she should give Esefa a chance before making any decisions. "Do you know much of the gods, Ranwif?" she asked.

"I am not sure I believe in them, Lady Qala."

"Ah, you should, my boy. You very much should." When he an-swered not, she added. "Perhaps I should pray that Esefa brings you love."

"That sort of thing is for young girls," he objected. "Did not your husband have different gods in his southern homeland?"

"I think it is too cold for them here," she responded. "We should seek elsewhere for our deities."

30

"I believe Benaro likes you," stated Sesa.

"Yet his eyes are often on you," Domi countered.

Zedos's nurse, who had given no indication she been listening until then, lifted her head. "That's young men for you. Can't stick with just one girl."

Sesa shrugged. "Not my type."

"Mine neither," said her friend. "I think I would like even our Ranwif better."

"Oh, not if I can get him first!"

"I guess the one of you who fails with Ranwif will have to take Benaro," spoke Qala for the first time. "Are they not the best of friends?"

"I but jested," claimed Domi. "Ranwif is far too obstinate and argumentative. You may have him," she told Sesa.

"You are completely right about him. But I see those as good qualities!"

Domi giggled. "Because you are like that yourself."

"Thank you!"

A rap came at the door. "Maybe that is our breakfast," spoke Domi. She opened it instead to the subject of their conversation, Ranwif. He nodded politely to the girls and reported, "Lord Corad has just ridden out again."

"How long will he stay?" asked Sesa. She sounded as if she wished he would depart soon; Qala understood why, as did her young captain.

"There is not much to draw him back to Sarowhem right now, I would think," said his sister. "He'll want to be home by Harvest Feast, of course."

"And to meet the Lady Vasema's parents there," Qala said. "It must be hard to lose a child."

She had expected a reaction from Sesa, but not what sort. It proved to be barely-controlled anger. "Some parents," hissed the girl, "don't really care about their child except to sell her where she doesn't wish to go."

Domi looked full of questions but she voiced none of them. Qala and Ranwif pretended they were elsewhere.

The nurse rose and said, "The little lord is sated. I'll be on my way, m'lady." She placed Zedos in his crib and departed as one of the kitchen helpers entered with stacked bowls of breakfast.

"Mush?" queried Ranwif, sniffing at the fare. "I think I'll head for the kitchen and find some bacon." He accompanied the scullion out the door.

"I like mush," stated Sesa. "When will Zedos be old enough to eat it?"

Qala had no exact idea about this, knowing only that babies did start eating solid food eventually. "He's nearly old enough to try," spoke the more knowledgeable Domi. "No need to rush our little crocodile."

Sesa scanned the bowls. "Honey? I need honey. Ah, there it is." She added only a small dollop to her cereal. Qala was quietly stirring yogurt into her own, and some of the stewed peaches.

It was Domi who said, "I agree with Ranwif. I need bacon."

"'Twill make you fat," warned Sesa. "Both of you."

"Ah, I can see us so, old and round, and Ranwif with a great un-kempt beard."

"Humph. If Rannie is going to end up like that then maybe I'm not interested in him after all."

A barely perceptible sound came from outside, like a stifled moan, and then a soft thud as if something bumped against the door. The girls had no idea what it was, might well have dismissed it, but Qala was at once on her feet and, a moment later, had her long-unused curved sword in her hand.

"What is wrong, mistress?" asked Sesa. Both young women stood, apprehensive but seemingly ready to face danger.

"I am fairly certain someone just killed the sentry," she replied. "Can you use weapons, Sesa?" Qala knew that Domi had received no training.

"I've handled a boar spear." Her eyes lit on the poker by the fire-place. "This will have to do," she said, grabbing it just as the door burst open.

"Take Zedos," she called to Domi and turned to do battle. Qala had no idea whom she might face but her first thought had been one of Xido's relatives come for her child. Only if she were dead!

But no, these were ordinary men, Sharshites. She threw herself at the first to enter, transfixing him before he knew what had happened and leaping over his body, her sword ready again. Sesa, being foolhardy perhaps, followed. She was a descendant of fighting men.

As was Domi, at least in part. She had bolted for Qala's bedchamber, Zedos in her arms. There would be no way to bar the door but it was better than remaining in the open.

Half a dozen men — five now — and several horses tethered close by. They should not have gotten this far! "There's the girl!" one shouted. "Grab her!"

The ruffian who attempted to carry out this order was laid out with an iron poker to the head. But there was no chance of resisting these armed men, not for long. Two engaged Qala while the others attempted to subdue their quarry. She kept them at bay only a few seconds before one had gotten behind Sesa and seized her arms.

"Hold!" came a cry, and men ran their way. It was enough to distract Sesa's captors a moment; she kicked out and wriggled free, as Ranwif and Augun rushed toward them, and some of the farmhands behind them. Qala glimpsed a pair of men running from the door of her quarters, calling the others to flee. She chased after, only to meet a booted foot from one of the riders. In a moment, five men thundered away; three others lay dead or wounded.

There had been two attackers Qala had not seen, who had entered her apartment while she battled outside. She ran in, to find Domi on the floor, bruised but not seriously harmed.

THE CROCODILE'S SON

"My lady! My lady!" she moaned. "They have taken the baby. Zedos is gone!"

Part III.
PRETENDERS

31.

It was too late to pursue. Qala lamented that she had no equesters in her service, truly no horsemen at all other than Ranwif.

But Ranwif and she must go after the kidnappers as soon as possible. Why would they take Zedos? She envisioned the torments she would inflict upon them if the child were harmed, torments only one who has ruled over a kingdom of pirates might imagine.

Domi was not greatly harmed. There was a great welt on her face, where one of the raiders had struck her down. For that alone, Qala would have inflicted much pain.

The stricken Sesa came to her. "It is all my fault, Qala," she wept. "I am not who I claimed."

"I have always recognized who you were, Vasema," she replied. "As did Ranwif. I willingly chose to offer my protection and that I will not regret."

Ranwif had stood brooding nearby. "Truly, it is I who must take the blame," said the boy. "I mentioned some vague suspicions about Sesa to Benaro weeks ago and he must have figured it out." With seeming reluctance, but not hesitating, he told them, "Benaro has friends with connections in the south."

"Find this man," ordered Qala, nodding toward Babo. The southerner motioned two men to follow him. No need; Benaro was already approaching, rapidly, along the dirt pathway.

"I am sorry, Ranwif," he choked out, and then dropped on his knees before the Muram woman. "Mistress Qala, my life is yours. I never knew — I never thought that somethin' like this would happen."

"Why was my son taken?" she demanded. Qala was in no mood for mercy.

"They offer to trade him for — her," he said, inclining his head toward Sesa. "They stopped at my cabin before ridin' south and told me this. And laughed when I said it was wrong."

"Fools, both of you," sighed Qala. "And I perhaps an even greater fool. We must ride after these men."

"I will go, my lady," asserted Sesa. "I am willing to exchange myself for Zedos."

Qala nodded curtly. "If it proves necessary, I shall not hesitate to do it. You will come too, Ranwif." She pondered her plan. "Yes, just the three of us shall ride."

"Four," came a voice. Corad approached, leading his horse. "A passerby on the road told me of what happened here and I rushed back. I am a fighting man, Qala, and I am at your service."

"Very well. We must be provisioned and on our way within the hour. You will want to send a message to Sarowhem before we go, I am sure. There is paper in my apartment."

The nobleman bowed slightly and stepped inside. To Ranwif and Vasema, Qala whispered, "We shall not inform Lord Corad of your identity, my girl, unless it is truly necessary. You remain Sesa. You both understand this?" They nodded their agreement though it was clear they did not understand her reasoning.

Horses were readied, bags filled with provisions, and they were off, riding south. To where? Perhaps all the way to the hold of the Pretender, if they received no other information.

Corad had met Sesa's presence with consternation. "When I heard you say three, I thought you included Ranwif's friend, not this girl. Why does she ride with us?"

"She rides well and knows woodcraft," was the only answer Qala would give him. Sesa had donned a loose, split skirt, and across her shoulder she carried a bow and quiver. That she also shot rather well with that bow, Qala had received numerous reports.

How had the gods permitted this? Hadn't they said they were keeping watch? It would be up to Qala herself to attend to her destiny, as ever.

To Domi, she had to entrust her estate. "You will obey Mistress Domi as you would me," she had announced before riding out. There was nothing more to be done there. One attacker had survived; he would keep.

They rode through that night, not yet ready to take time for rest. But what was the point? There would be no catching up to the men ahead, men who knew the countryside as well as or better than Ranwif this time.

"We must halt and allow the horses to rest," spoke Corad, shortly after dawn. Qala was of no mind to delay her pursuit but recognized the truth of this. She reined in her horse and dismounted without a word.

No words were exchanged during their quick, cold meal either. Each had his or her own thoughts, it seemed, thoughts none were ready to share. They rode on through the day, moving southward through ever-emptier wooded lands, resting but a few minutes, now and again. That could not be kept up, not by rider nor by steed. Indeed, the horses had already been pushed too far.

"We will camp here," Qala said at last, holding up a hand to signal the halt. "No longer than necessary."

32.

It was a Muram patrol. They could have shown themselves and offered an explanation, but Ranwif advised otherwise. Corad concurred. "It would delay us." At best — far worse things could come of meeting a band of soldiers in the wilderness. The group remained concealed in the brush until the Mura had passed.

"Further along, we would have a greater likelihood of meeting some of Flawum's men," said Ranwif. "Both groups tend to avoid confronting each other, when possible, but there is the occasional skirmish."

"The empire hasn't the resources to occupy these lands and root out any rebels," came, to the surprise of all, from Sesa. "So they let things go on as they are."

"You know something of politics, girl," said Corad. From the look he gave her, perhaps he didn't quite approve of that.

Sesa shrugged. "'Tis but common sense."

He also did not approve of her not speaking to him with more deference, Qala sensed. Corad would not press that; there were more important considerations at the moment.

"Let's move on," said Qala.

Ranwif followed her back onto the narrow pathway, peering at the ground. "That troop would have trampled any tracks. We've even less chance of finding them now."

"We know where they are headed and you know the way. Take us there!"

"Yes, my lady." The four rode on, through the day and past the sunset, before weariness demanded a halt. They moved well away from the trail to avoid detection, and lit no fire, camping on the edge of a hidden field of maize, all dry dead stalks at this season. Qala grew maize but it was something of a newcomer to Sharshite lands, having been introduced from the south by Muram traders. "We won't see whoever planted this," said Ranwif. "Folk around here know it's best to keep out of sight."

"They wasted cattle feed by not cutting it," was Corad's only comment. Sesa nodded in agreement, but spoke not.

"I am going to go in there a way for some privacy," announced Qala. She hoped that her churning bowels would cooperate — all this riding on short rations was leaving her at less than her best and the Mur wanted to be at her best. She *needed* to be at her best. Where was Zedos? Was he safe? The knot in her guts had as much to do with her fears for her son as anything else, she knew.

"I'll allow you your privacy, my Qala," came a velvet voice from somewhere among the cornstalks. "I've come to offer our apologies."

"Lenco?" She felt absurd, squatting there while conversing with a god.

"I could probably help you with that," he said. "There are spells — hmm, no not that one. Not on a human. Well, maybe best to leave it to nature."

"Do you have knowledge of my son?" Why was the fool of a deity talking about her bowels?

"Ah, well, we are fairly certain the boy is unharmed. As to his exact whereabouts — you know we are limited when we enter your world and take human shape."

"Yes. Xit was so."

"Exactly. And Xido is better at being human than the rest of us. He likes to walk among you." There was momentary silence, save for a light breeze rustling through the dry stalks. "We weren't paying attention, busy with the things of our own world. Budo, too, so we weren't concerned about him, and let our guard down. Who were those men who took my nephew?"

Qala grunted. Ah. That was better. "Followers of a rebel leader to the south. They want to exchange Zedos for another." She wiped herself with a dry leaf from the maize and stood, straightening her kilt. "I am willing to do that."

"All done?" The cornstalks parted and the lean, dark god emerged. "The girl who rides with you, I assume."

"Yes. The Pretender, Flawum, wants her as his wife. It would help his legitimacy in the eyes of the Sharshites, he thinks." Or so Ranwif had told her.

"The one who used to hold the Earth Stone. Xido stole that, didn't he? That's the rumor." He chuckled; even his chuckles were melodious. "Xido has a history of leaving places with other people's property."

"So did I," she reminded him. "All I want right now is my son. Will you help?"

"Of course, my lady. That is why I am here." The sardonic Lenco disappeared and a far more solemn god spoke. "We promised to watch out for the lad and failed in our duty. This lays an heavy obligation on Mawa and me."

"On Budo, too," came another, thicker voice. "We work together this time, Brother." A shadow emerged from a place of shadow, and became the god. He held up a massive cudgel and shook it. "I will smash heads!"

"Let us hope that is not necessary," replied Lenco. "We should go home and make plans, eh?" He bowed toward Qala. "Know that we will not forget our obligations this time, my lady." Both deities stepped into the darkened ways between the rows of maize, disappearing.

Qala returned to her comrades, already wrapped in blankets and doz-ing off. They must be away again in a few hours; best she grab a little sleep herself, if she could. The Mur felt considerably better after her vis-it to the corn field.

33.

Qala dreamed of a starving Zedos, crying for milk. She woke of a sudden and sat up.

The former queen of pirates was not one to cry. At that moment she wished she might, to bawl as she had when her love had been slain those many years ago. She had been but a child then, truly, but taking revenge had changed that. Qala had not wept since.

She shook, keeping herself from it now. It was Sesa who came and placed an arm around her. "We shall get him back, my lady." The girl trembled, close to tears of her own. "I was wicked to run away and cause all this."

"I have led a life of wickedness," whispered Qala. "Must I pay for it so?"

No. She would not give way to despair, though that serpent had always slept near her heart. The former pirate had, at last, something to live for. Qala would not let it be taken from her. She rose and announced, "Time to move."

It was not yet light but they had rested long enough. The horses looked able to go on, though their forage was sparse here in this autumn woodland. The four searchers saddled up, not stopping for a meal, and set out. They could eat in the saddle.

"It would be best," spoke Ranwif, after some time, if we enter the Pretender's lands as someone other than ourselves. Our identities could be revealed later, if need be." He looked directly toward Corad, riding abreast. "This is especially true of you, sir. At best, you would be held for a considerable ransom." He did not say what might happen at worst, but they could all picture various unpleasant scenarios.

"You are known, are you not?" asked Qala.

"By some. Best if I use my own name, in case I am recognized, but volunteer nothing further. You," he said, turning to Sesa, "are my new bride, the farm girl I just ran away with."

She readily fell in with this plan. "Then my name is good enough, too." Her eyes went to their companions. "They'll be more difficult."

"Captives, maybe?" conjectured Corad.

Sesa laughed. "No one would believe that!"

"Traders," stated Qala. "We are close enough in age to be husband and wife, a pair of merchants on our way to — well, we're going somewhere." Corad's expression suggested some skepticism about the idea. "Well, I am not that much older than you!"

Ranwif made no comment on that, but said, "You could be heading to the southern coasts to take ship across the channel to Lorj. Smuggler craft cross regularly."

"Indeed?" asked Corad. "My friend Captain Nedos should know of this."

"I am sure he knows who pays his bribes, sir," was Ranwif's answer. Corad could find no response to that. "Anyway, we have fallen in with each other somewhere along the way south. Traveling companions and nothing more."

"Good enough," said Qala. "You have the makings of an excellent outlaw, my boy. I shall be Tes and my husband, um, Domos." Corad chuckled at his alias, a masculine variant of his half-sister's name.

And Qala wondered why the first name to pop into her head was the one she used as a young woman, before she rose to rule among the corsairs. Ah, at least it was not her real name — none of them would ever know that.

The girl who had worn it died long ago, hadn't she? She rode on in silence, but her mood was better now. The assurances of Lenco had much to do with it, just the knowledge that Zedos was alright. Those who took him would take care of the boy, wouldn't they? At least while he remained of use to them.

Any exchange would have to made with care, thus the secrecy about Vasema's identity. It wouldn't do to ride in announcing who she was. Wouldn't Corad be surprised? The man had ridden without question, with no knowledge of her plan, only pledging to aid her. He was a good man, Corad. His intended bride could have done far, far worse.

For a time, they paralleled a rocky, unnavigable river. "It flows into the Chas a bit upstream from your place," Corad informed Qala. Then they veered away from it again. There seemed less point in rushing on now, and they felt safe lighting a fire to cook small game that fell to the arrows of Sesa. A low range of hills lay somewhere ahead where the Pretender had his court, a divide between those waters that flowed north to the Chas and those that went south to the Lesser Sea.

Villages began to appear, welcome after the lonely, empty lands they had crossed. These little towns all paid homage to Flawum, the man they called Ri of Sharsh, their king. What troops they passed were the Pretender's men as well, men who asked them their business and, satisfied, let them pass. It seemed likely they knew nothing of this business of kidnapping and runaway brides.

A cold wind blew at their backs. Autumn was following them south, and beckoning winter to follow. "It's milder on the other side of the hills, as a rule," Ranwif told them. "And hardly cold at all on the shores of the sea. If it weren't a lawless wilderness it would be most excellent place to live."

"The soil is poor there," interjected Sesa. "Or so I have read." Ranwif knew nothing of such things and, moreover, did not care.

Corad, not so. "Sand and scrub, it is said. Lorj itself, across the channel, is not so much better."

"Yet they cultivate wide fields in the valley of the Erd," the girl replied and the two fell a bit away from their companions to discuss agriculture for the next hour, as they rode on.

Said Corad in an aside to Qala, that evening, "I said, jesting in main part, I would just as soon take a farm girl to wife. Were she one such as your Sesa, I think I would readily go through with it." He smiled, shaking his head. "No time to think of such things right now! She is Ranwif's anyway, is she not?"

"That you would have to ask the girl herself, my friend," replied the

113

Muram woman. "Now sleep. I intend to ride again before dawn."

"Yes, yes." She heard him pulling at his blanket, trying to make himself comfortable, before he muttered, "She is too argumentative, anyway, and has no respect for her betters."

The next sound to come from Corad was soft snoring.

34.

"This is easier when there is less light," said the slender woman. "It's all just a trick, you know, a pulling in of shadows to conceal us as we pop into your world."

"Then they don't actually have anything to do with the way you, um, come to our world?"

"Nothing at all, Qala. Ah, don't look so disappointed!" Mawa's laugh came quick and ready, but was displaced as quickly by a serious mood. "I have seen your son. He is in this Flawum's deteriorating castle, and well cared for. They even found a wet nurse for him."

"Couldn't you do anything? Couldn't you, ah, take him through one of those doors of yours?"

"I could but, unfortunately, not completely. Part of little Zedos would remain tethered to this world and must, in time, pull him back." Mawa gave a rather exaggerated shrug. Qala approved of the ways it made the goddess' body move. "To exactly the same spot he left."

"Oh! That would be no good."

"The truth is, I am also tethered. Understand, my Qala, I am not entirely here in your world, but part of me remains connected to my home. To break that connection completely, as did Xido, is a serious undertaking." She frowned, just a little, before going on. "And one only gods can accomplish. I think, more than anything else, that is what makes us gods."

"Are you talking to yourself, Qala?" came Corad's voice.

Qala gave her companion a glance. Mawa nodded an approval. "No, we have a visitor." The man blundered his way through the bushes to them.

"Oh, Lady Mawa." He gave her a bow. "Best not tell the others of this though, eh?"

"Not unless there is a need," was Qala's opinion. Mawa seemed to concur. "I suppose they are ready to be on the road."

"We have no more we need to discuss," spoke the dark goddess.

"You will see us again." She looked around, seemingly miffed. "I need a shady spot to do this properly."

"My lady," said Corad, with some embarrassment, "should you visit again you might want to, um, cover up a bit. I am not one to complain but it is the custom here and you would not want to stand out."

"As if my looks wouldn't be enough?"

"You could pass for a southerner," was Qala's opinion. A very nice-looking southerner. "Xit did."

"Oh, very well. I suppose I could find a shirt. Or borrow one of yours," she said to Qala. "We're close in size." She walked to a massive oak, and saying, "I'll disappear the easy way," slipped behind its trunk.

"Are your friendly gods going to help us?" asked the Sharshite noble-man as they headed back to their camp.

"I don't know. I mean, I don't know if they really are much help but I think they are going to try. They can spy where we could not."

"That is something," Corad said. "We are near the Pretender's keep according to Ranwif."

"That is good, husband mine. We must remember to play our roles at all times from now on."

"It comes not natural to me, my lady. I have trouble playing even myself."

"I must also learn more of your Sharshic tongue," said Qala. "Keep up my education." She had been learning more words as they had ridden, adding to what Sharshic she had already picked in her tenure at Melawhem, both to while the time and better prepare. It would be useful knowledge when she returned home, too, but she would need much more instruction.

Then they were off again, the village beside Flawum's manor to be their next stop. Qala had no true plan; it was possible they would be recognized at once and then all that could be done was hand Vasema over and trust the kidnappers to return her son.

She would prefer to rescue Zedos and use the girl only as a last resort. Sesa was probably the least recognizable individual in their group, although her would-be abductors had seen her. Qala called a halt and the four riders bunched up for a final conference.

"We must cover ourselves as much as is practical," he said. "The weather is cool so it should not seem suspicious. Wear a hood when you can, Sesa, and I shall too." She looked at the men. "Just the beards you two have grown on this journey should help." Indeed, it quite changed the boy. "I have decided on a change," she continued. "We shall go in separately, Domos and I first. If we get too much attention, it will make it all the easier for Sesa and Ranwif to slip by unrecognized"

A cottage was spied by their road, a road grown wide, in the mid-afternoon. Others lay beyond it. "We had best split here," said Ranwif. "We'll let you ride ahead for, oh, half an hour?" He grinned at Sesa. "Maybe longer if we find a tavern."

Corad seemed disapproving but Qala said, "Stopping for refreshment is not a bad idea. It makes you look all the more like ordinary travelers."

She and the nobleman rode ahead. "Cobblestones," remarked Corad, as the dirt road gave way to pavement. "I didn't expect such sophistication here."

"Ranwif has been filling me in on the history of this place. It was prosperous once, when trade flowed through here. That all dried up after the Muram conquest."

"I should know more of my nation's history." Corad looked down the winding way. "Those towers must be the Pretender's keep."

Qala almost lost her temper. "Flawum's keep," she hissed. "Don't call him that here!"

Corad spoke no more, which both felt was wise. Substantial timber-framed buildings stood on either side of the street, many rising two stories. Shops, some, or inns, but most seemed residences. Most also seemed a bit shabby. This village was prosperous once but no more.

THE CROCODILE'S SON

A high wall, a gate hanging wide, a courtyard beyond. "This is it," spoke Qala, and urged her mount forward. Corad followed.

35.

One piece of information had somehow failed to find its way to Qala, even though her three companions were aware of it: Sharshic only was spoken in the Pretender's compound. It was good that she had learned a few phrases, but Qala would still have difficulty following what was being said and whether Corad — who spoke the language perfectly — was sticking to the plan.

Best she feign compete ignorance of the language, eh? Well, Corad and the guards were laughing. That was good. To Qala, he whispered, "Flawum is through with holding court today. We're to be put up in the keep for the night." Which was a polite way of saying they were prisoners, she suspected.

It was hardly a cell to which they were shown, but a well-appointed bedchamber. Yes, the furnishings were old and the worse for wear. "I gave them the story you crafted," Corad told her when they were alone. "Husband and wife, traders down on our luck, trying to make it to the coast and cross over to Lorj with smuggler friends." He gave her a wry grin. "It's a good thing you knew the names of a smuggler or two."

Qala bounced on the lumpy bed a couple times and shrugged. "Was my being Muram a problem?"

"Not so much when I said you were from across the sea. I've heard that the Pre — er, the Ri has certain arrangements with some of the old kingdoms."

The onetime pirate nodded. Such rumors had reached her in her former life. "This is the better side of the bed," she decided. "You stick to the other one." Qala had absolute trust in Corad's honor — far more than in her own — and so knew he would behave as a gentleman. "I wonder where Zedos is in this pile of rocks."

"As much as it tempts, I do not think we should go exploring. We'll find him, Qala, and get both of you back to Melawhem." He still did not pry into the reasons for the abduction.

"That is my intention." Then, practical as ever, she said, "I wonder if we could explore for some food. We should have stopped at a tavern too!"

"If there is a guard nearby, I'll ask." Corad opened the door, peering both ways down the hallway. "We seem to have been deserted," he said. "I guess they think we aren't dangerous."

"Right now, I'm inclined to agree. I'm too tired and hungry to knife anyone."

"I thought they took your knife."

"Not the one I strapped to my thigh. Do you think I'm the sort of woman to carry only one knife?" A rap came on the door. "Ah, perhaps I'll have the chance to use it!"

It proved to be a guardsman with their supper. He and Corad exchanged a few words in Sharshic. "He apologized that it was late and cold," Corad told his companion. "Let's see what we have."

Late and cold it might be, but the meal was substantial, cold beef and sweet cakes and dried fruit. There was a bland wine to wash it down. "I wonder if this is a local vintage," spoke Corad.

"Lorjam, I'd say. Smuggled up from the coast." Qala had imbibed her share of cheap wine from the sun-baked vineyards of northern Lorj. "Maybe I should put in some vines at Melawhem."

"We've had trouble with diseases," came Corad's somewhat sleepy reply. "The guard said to just set these outside the door when we were done. Is there a — oh, there." He had spied the chamber pot.

"I'll set them out. Let me in when you're ready." Qala carried the tray and empty bowls out into the hall, and placed them against the stone wall. There had been plaster over those stones once, and bits of it remained here and there. It might have been a mural; who could tell? It was dark. A single lantern burnt well down the corridor. Shadows — she almost expected one of Xido's relatives to step out into the open but it did not happen.

Later, she tossed on the uncomfortable bed, Corad snoring beside her, and thought of her son, somewhere in this building. She listened, hoping to catch his lusty squall arising, calling to his mother from a nearby room. If she could but speak to someone here, a maid or scullion. They would know if a baby were about the place. Surely one or two would speak Muram, or she could stumble through enough Sharshic to be understood, Qala told herself, as she finally slipped into sleep.

It was Corad, and Corad only who was called to be interviewed in the morning. Or, we should say, Domos was called. At least a decent breakfast had been brought first, though the fried eggs were only luke-warm. They must be a good distance from the kitchen.

That or the guards dawdled along the way. Qala was left to herself, with little to amuse her. Why not explore? she asked. She'd just be a poor lost little woman, looking for her husband, if anyone saw her.

Out she slipped and down the hallway — and directly into a detachment of guardsmen coming about the corner. She pressed against the wall, uncertain of her course. Surely they had seen her.

Yet they acted as if she were not right in front of them. "Hold still, my lady. I have called shadows around us so none can see we are here."

"Budo?" she whispered.

"Shh!" The men marched on by, noticing nothing. "There," said the god. "All safe now."

"Thank you. Do — do you know where my son is?"

"The king of this place keeps him in his room. It is, um, that way." He pointed and then furrowed his brow. "I think. Down the stairs. Of that I am sure. Flawum does not like stairs."

Qala sighed. She might as well return to her room and wait for Corad. Budo walked beside her, not stomping along as one might expect of a fellow his size, but with a light and athletic step. "We will get your son back, my lady. I promise this, I, Budo the Boar."

Did Budo in fact turn into a pig? wondered Qala. He did not look much like one but then Xido didn't really resemble a crocodile. And she didn't even want to think about the Spider, Mawa. She was thankful the

121

god left her at her door and faded into the gloom of the passageway. Nothing to do but wait.

36

"They brought in the youngsters while I was there," reported Corad. "Ranwif was recognized, apparently, and is welcome in Flawum's keep. The old boy even treated him as a noble, having him announced with the title of Mor." He shook his head, his expression one of amusement. "I think he was disappointed in Ranwif's choice of wife."

"He is lame, isn't he? Marana told me something about that."

"Suffers bouts of gout. He looked to be doing well enough right now." The Sharshite seemed wrapped in his own thoughts for a few seconds. "Flawum's not really old, of course. I would guess around your age, my lady, or a little more. Certainly less than four tens of years."

"That is a total at which I have yet to arrive," said Qala. She thought it must be about three years away but was uncertain, nor did she know the day of her birth.

"My mother has proclaimed she will never reach it. Flawum does want to meet you. I had to tell him you were the one with the contacts among the smugglers, which was the truth." He picked at a bit of bread left from their lunch. Corad had not seemed hungry and Qala suspected he had eaten before returning. "But I think he is interested in attractive women as a general thing."

He smiled at his comrade. "Do not again deny you are one, Friend Qala. You put girls half your age to shame." This, Qala did not believe but let it pass. "He will call for us in his private chambers sometime. Maybe this evening, maybe tomorrow."

"That is good, for I have learned that Zedos is kept there." There were many questions in the look Corad gave her. She answered one of them. "I spoke to someone in the hall while you were gone." Many other questions had gone unanswered. Qala thought it was time that changed.

"I should have told you this before," she began. "About why this Flawum's men took my son. They believe that I have the Lady Vasema and wish to trade for her." That she in truth did have the girl, Qala was not about to reveal. Not unless it were truly necessary.

Corad took this in calmly. "I had assumed they were holding him for ransom but did not know the price. Vasema is surely dead. We must convince him of this."

"I fear that would make him no more likely to hand over Zedos."

"Maybe not. Could you pay a ransom of the more ordinary sort, were it demanded?" Before she could answer, he went on, "No, my family is to blame for all of this. I pledge our wealth to you."

"If I steal the boy back that will not be necessary." Corad did not appear to think that likely but held his tongue.

It was not that evening they were called to Flawum but surprisingly early the next day. "The Ri does not hold court until sometime around late morning, usually," a functionary explained as she led the way. She spoke in Muram as a courtesy to Qala, the first time she had heard her own language spoken by those who dwelt within these walls. "That does not mean he won't rise early to attend to his royal duties." She smiled at her own words. "Fairly early."

The woman wore a long, shapeless gown, once purple, perhaps, but faded to a mottled warm brown. As Lady-in-Waiting to the Queen had she been announced to them but, so far as either knew, there was no queen.

Flawum was exercising when they were ushered into his antechamber, languidly performing shallow squatting movements in the middle of the room. A threadbare carpet was beneath his slipper-shod feet; many mismatched tapestries covered up the walls. Qala gave the man a look but he was not what interested her. Zedos would be somewhere in this apartment!

"I must stay fit!" he stated, speaking also in Muram. "My doctor says it might help prevent the return of the gout. The blood-flow or something of the sort — but you don't care about all of that!" The Pretender could certainly use any exercise he got, thought Qala. He was not fat, particularly, but certainly soft.

"Sit, sit," he told them. "We don't follow the protocol of the throne room here." The would-be monarch eyed Qala. "You're from the Mu-ram kingdoms, aren't you? Which one?"

"Tesra, sir. That's how I got my name." This was actually true — not that she had been born there but she had spent some time.

"Oh, I've never had a Tesran here before!"

"We sail from Esadon. Tesra is no sort of a port anymore, your majesty." This, too, was fact. The greatest city of the world, once, was a backwater these days, a metropolis of crumbling ruins.

Flawum nodded absently. "Enough of a workout," he decided, and flopped onto the nearest divan. "So you need to make it down to the coast, do you? There are dangers crossing to Lorj but I am sure you know that!" He turned abruptly to an aide, asking, "Where is our other visitor?"

"With the child, your highness," came the man's reply, almost as a whisper. "He did ask to see him."

"Oh, right. Get him out here, will you?" His attention returned to his guests. "I have a trader from the southern isles here. He looked too much like that scoundrel of a wizard who robbed me last year! Or that's the year before, now, isn't it? I almost ordered him executed just for that!"

A slender, brown man in a long, loose tunic, striped blue and white, entered. "Ho, Lingo, come meet my other visitors. You might wish to travel south with them."

"Perhaps, Great One," the god politely answered, bowing deeply. "The infant does, indeed, appear to be of my people."

Flawum shook his head. "It has not been adequately explained to me why he was at a Sharshite manor. I wonder if maybe they took the wrong child!"

"That is nothing I would know, sir," murmured Lenco.

"Nor any of your concern," added the aide.

125

"Most true. None of this has anything to do with our guests," agreed the Pretender. He turned his attention again to Qala and Corad. "You had little of value with you, besides your horses. Maybe I should just turn you out."

"Oh, Great One," spoke Lenco, "if these worthy travelers choose to accompany me, truly would I attend to any incidental expenses."

Flawum smiled, nodding his head in approval. "Excellent. Excuse me now, it is time for my bath. I have worked up quite a sweat!"

All three visitors were ushered from the room, again accompanied by the Queen's Lady. "You have the freedom of the keep and of the village now," she told them, with a faint smile. "As long as his highness is as-sured he will make a profit, you are his welcome guests."

Lenco accompanied his mortal friends as far as the door to their room. "Alas, the gold I shall pay to our host is tethered to another realm and will disappear from his treasury after a time. It is to be hoped we shall disappear first!" He bowed and added, "I too am tethered after a fashion, and feel the need to slip back to my own world. Expect my return."

The god walked a short way down the hall, pulling shadows about him as he went, and vanished.

37.

"No one at the court seems to know what is going on with their ransom scheme. They are not even sure if their demands have been delivered. So Flawum is going to send another messenger to make certain." The four who had ridden south together were once again gathered, now in Ranwif's chambers. Ranwif and Sesa's, since they posed as man and wife. It varied little from the one Qala and Corad occupied.

"I could advise sending you as a messenger," continued Ranwif. "They assume I am now outlawed in Muram lands, or I would be asked."

"There's no reason for me to leave," replied the nobleman. "Not that I can see a way to do anything here."

Ranwif nodded. "It doesn't look good."

"What a pair!" scoffed Sesa. "We might has well have left you behind."

Corad bristled; he was unhappy already with the way things were going. "And what is your plan, girl?"

"My plan is to make a plan," she snapped back at him, "rather than sitting and moaning."

Qala was thinking similar thoughts. As one used to leading, she knew better than to express them aloud. "Then a plan we shall make," she stated. "The question is whether we can expect any help from Zedos's relatives."

"Relatives, my lady?" asked Ranwif. He knew nothing of them, and Sesa only a little more.

"I believe you have met one of them," the older man told him. "Lingo."

"That trader? Oh, is he of your late husband's family, my lady?"

Sesa snickered, knowing that husband a fabrication. "I'd best go through the whole story for them," sighed Qala. It was two pitchers of wine later that she finished.

There are no more secrets here, thought the Muram woman. Except that Corad still knew not Sesa's identity. She was not quite ready to reveal that.

"Do you think they are watching us now?" wondered Sesa.

Qala shrugged. "Who could say? I do hope they check on Zedos sometimes." She also wished they would report on him.

There came a heavy knocking at the door. A soldier of the keep stood there. "The Ri will speak with you." His eyes swept across the group. "All four." The man stepped aside and Flawum entered, accompanied by the woman with whom they had spoken earlier. The soldier and another took up positions on either side of the door, as she closed it behind herself and their liege.

"I hope you don't mind me intruding," spoke the Pretender of Sharsh. "I was told you were all together so it seemed a good time. You have all met the Lady Hasala, have you not?" The lady-in-waiting to the late queen acknowledged them with a slight nod of the head.

She remained poised by the entryway while Flawum took one of the chairs. "Please, sit," he said. There were not sufficient chairs so Sesa perched on the bed. "You are recently come from the north," he continued, to no one in particular. But it applied to all of them.

"I only seek news," he said. "We hoped to have my promised bride, the Lady Vasema, here soon. We sent messages anyway, asking that she be sent."

"Does she know she is to be your bride?" asked Sesa. Everyone, except maybe Flawum, noticed she used no title of respect.

The man dismissed her question. "It was decided long ago. Something about alliances and connections, you know? I need a wife. And an heir, an heir with the right, um, pedigree. That sounds rather awful, doesn't it?" No one was going to answer that so Flawum went on.

"I regret having no children but might yet remedy that. My first wife died, you know, and I never remarried." He sat for quite some time before saying aught else. "I miss her."

"I will pray to Esefa that you again find love, your majesty," spoke

Qala. She hoped the goddess would not mind her using her name so!

"If this Vasema is delivered to me, I suppose I must marry her." Flawum seemed less than enthusiastic about the prospect. "I'd rather marry someone else." He did not say whom but his eyes strayed to his late wife's lady-in-waiting. "There would be no hope of a dowry from a family in the empire. I'd only be getting that pedigree."

"Then would not any noble Sharshite bride do, sir?" asked Corad.

"That's what I tell my ministers! And I do not approve of this kidnapping business they've been up to."

"Maybe, sir, you need new ministers."

"You have heard what news I had, your highness," said Ranwif, apparently thinking this a good time to nudge the discourse in a different direction. "It was only rumored that she was in vicinity of the estate your men raided."

"And the rest of us have heard even less, sir," added Qala. "We were but travelers on the road."

Flawum shook his head. "Yet the men claimed she was there and they almost had her."

"They almost had someone," broke in Sesa. "How did they know it was the right woman?"

Flawum looked annoyed this time, whether at her familiarity or at the questions she posed, none could tell. "We must go," he said, rising. "I thank you for your company." The Pretender suddenly laughed. "You had no news but I think I learned some things anyway."

He left; the Lady Hasala, however, allowed her gaze to linger for a moment on the group. Then she, too, passed out the door.

38.

"Hasala is a handsome woman," remarked Qala, once she and her sham husband had returned to their quarters.

Corad shut the door and turned to her. "Yes. I think she was looking me over."

"Oh, no, Corad, it was I she was giving the eye."

"Neither of us, I think, shall have the opportunity to find out." He chuckled. "Unless we kidnapped the lady and took her back with us."

"If the Lady Vasema is never found, she might be an excellent substitute."

Corad's laugh came louder this time. "As I told Flawum, any noble Sharshite bride would do." Then he thought more fully, and a frown replace his laughter. "Noble she certainly is or she would not hold her position. But a noble of an outlawed family, also certainly. It would not be possible."

He actually considered it, thought Qala. However, she still believed it was she in whom the woman was interested. Hasala *was* attractive, in a somewhat typical Sharshite way, and still young — perhaps in her mid-twenties, surely no older than Corad. Did she imagine a resemblance to the goddess Esefa?

Maybe the goddess was making good on her promise. She could hope, couldn't she? But Qala had far more important concerns.

"Where are you, my lady?" asked Corad. "You seemed to go on a very long voyage."

"And I have returned. It's time to eat, isn't it?"

"Past time, I think. I'll run downstairs and get us something." Now they had the freedom of the keep, they were expected to find their own meals.

"I thought he would never leave," said Mawa, as soon as Corad was out the door. She had taken his advice and wore a reasonably modest tunic now. Quite unnecessary, felt Qala, as she was the only one likely to be seeing the goddess — and she would prefer to see more of her.

But no time for such thoughts now! "Have you news, my lady?" she asked.

"Of sorts. We've been working on a plan." Mawa took a place on the end of the bed. "Maybe more an idea than a plan. Come, sit." She patted the place beside her.

"One of us can draw a being here that can take the place of Zedos. A changeling."

Qala took a seat beside the goddess, saying, "Would it fool those who hold my child?"

"It should. A little dark child; that's all most of them see." She turned to face the Muram woman. "But you would still need to reach Zedos and spirit him away somehow for it to work."

"Oh, is that all?" Qala could not keep at least a touch of sarcasm from creeping into her voice.

Which Mawa either ignored or did not note. "We can help you with it. You know we have ways to conceal and confuse. In time, the changeling would be pulled back to the world from which we call it. Enough time to get away, we would hope."

It all seemed too far-fetched. Qala was of half a mind to just go to Flawum, reveal Sesa's identity, and hope he would return her son. Instead, must she place hope in these unreliable aunts and uncles of the child?

She would have to think further on these things before making any decision. Perhaps ask advice, as well; she trusted all her companions' counsel but would, ultimately, choose their course herself.

Meanwhile, it would be good to learn more of these gods and what they could do. "Why," Qala asked, "could not Xido do the things you and your brothers accomplish with such seeming ease?"

She was not sure Mawa would answer for a while. "Because Xido chose to enter entirely this world, becoming completely human," the goddess said at last. "It diminishes our power to do so. We could not pull things of other worlds so readily to ourselves, such as those shadows we use so much. Nor could we move back and forth between those worlds as we do. Xido cut himself off from the power of his home and became no different than a powerful sorcerer of your world — except with the knowledge of a god."

"Then how will he return to your world? Must he wander here forever?" Qala did not at all like that thought. She might never have loved the father of her son, but she was fond of him and cared about his fate.

"No, my Qala, fear not for my brother. Once he chose to return to his crocodile shape he began the journey home, for he had put aside being a mortal man. Some day he will return to us when he grows weary of swimming the seas." She laughed. "It might be tomorrow, it might be an hundred years. Who knows with our Xido?"

"I am gladdened to know this, Mawa." She felt he should ask then, "You would not do such a thing, would you?"

"All of us have at some time. Maybe I shall again some day. Who knows with Mawa, either?" She lay back on the bed, with her hands clasped behind her head. "In truth, the further we get from the temporary doors we create, the more difficult things become for us. We do not wander too far from them. For one who takes on the mortal form, that no longer matters."

"But you pay a different price." Qala settled down beside her, propping herself on an elbow so she might look upon this goddess, her friend, her lover. "I have missed your company."

"And I yours. But stuffy old Corad will be back soon."

Qala's sigh was not meant at all seriously. "I guess there is nothing we can do about that."

"We could invite him to join us, hmm? No, I know he is not the sort. Too bad, though," mused Mawa, "he is rather well-formed." She sat up. "And you have too many other things to think of right now. I shall go." She cocked her head at the Mur and asked, "Would you like to see it without the illusions?"

"I —" Qala wasn't sure if she should. Maybe such things were better cloaked in shadow. "If you wish."

It was as though a thousand different shapes all tried to exist at the same point. Or no, it was one shape, wasn't it, seen from a multitude of different angles? But not a woman, a swollen spider, or so it seemed for a brief moment, so brief Qala could not be certain, as each image twisted away into nothing.

Yes, such things were indeed better cloaked in shadow.

39.

"He seems more than some merchant," spoke Hasala. "And you — you do not act like his wife, Tes."

I might as well give up, Qala told herself. This Sharshite woman truly had been looking at Corad. She had hopes, what with Lady Hasala being not so young and attached to no man, that she might like women. Hopes for herself? No, not really — the noblewoman was rather pretty, if one went for pale ladies with curls of gold and nervous ways. Qala did not.

She wouldn't have minded a dalliance, of course, but it was where the woman could have gotten her that mattered. Hasala had the freedom of Flawum's rooms, the rooms where her son was held.

"Domos is of an aristocratic heritage," she said. That was true, after all. "Another of those families driven from their homes by the empire." And that was not true.

"As my own," came Hasala's subdued response. "Those who yet live."

"And Domos and I — we are in truth naught but business partners. The claim of marriage only simplifies matters when we travel." If the lady-in-waiting was interested in Corad, she would open up the path to him. "I do not really prefer men," she murmured, as though it were some deep secret.

"Ah. Oh, you were —" Hasala blushed when she realized she had been quite oblivious of Qala's advances only minutes before. "I am, uh, not —"

"So I realized, my lady. But why is so lovely a woman without a man?" Qala helped herself to more of the sweet, pale-red wine and made sure to refill her companion's cup too. The woman was already talkative and it wouldn't hurt to further lubricate her tongue.

"I have been waiting for one man." The Sharshite woman snickered. "The lady-in-waiting has been waiting too long!"

Flawum was Qala's guess. And there appeared to be an unrequited desire on the Pretender's part, as well. She would not say this straight out, but the subject could be approached by another way. "Lady-in-waiting — you served the Ri's late wife?"

A somber nod. "She was my cousin and I came to court with her when she was to be wed. Flawum truly loved his queen and was devastated when the grippe took her away from him. It took him long to show an interest in anything again, or even to leave his bed."

"And you served him all through that time," Qala hazarded. It proved a good guess.

"I did and — and I fell in love with him." There were tears in those green eyes. Qala felt like smacking the fool — or at least giving her a good shake — but managed to find a modicum of empathy within herself. "But I am done with him!" Hasala declared. "I am going to run away with your husband!" A tipsy giggle followed.

So Corad represented only an escape. No, he was more than that; the man's solid presence was just the thing to attract this woman at this time, a rock anyone might think to cling to. "We will have to get the opinion of Domos on that, Lady Hasala," said Qala. "But know that nothing you have told me will be repeated."

"Oh, thank you, Tes," gushed the noblewoman, perhaps realizing she had been a little too talkative. "None of your secrets will go beyond this room either."

"That is good," said Qala, rising. "I shall leave you to your siesta, my lady, and return to my quarters. I thank you for your hospitality."

Of course, all that Hasala had told her *would* be repeated to her fellow conspirators here in the keep of the Pretender. It had been useful to take lunch with the Queen's Lady; Qala had thought that she had manipulated Hasala into inviting her, at the start. She realized now that the noblewoman had been working toward the same thing, but for quite different reasons!

Whatever the reasons, it could still provide her a way into Flawum's apartment, a way to her son.

Corad was snoring on the bed when she slipped into their room. As many another Sharshite, he took his nap time seriously. It was a custom Qala was unlikely to adopt; she had trouble enough sleeping at night. Well, she had the freedom of this place, so she would walk.

Was Lenco about somewhere? He seemed to have been accepted as a traveling merchant by the authorities here so he must have lodging. But he wouldn't remain in his room, would he? The god would open a door into this world when his presence was needed. Still, it would be useful to know where that room lay.

How long, too, could he dawdle here and not raise suspicion? All of them were only supposed to be passing through. They must act soon. Qala knew better than to stop a servant and ask of the trader, Lingo. They would either not speak Muram or pretend that they did not, and she was reluctant to reveal any knowledge of Sharshic, however meager. Maybe Ranwif would know something.

It was in the Pretender's stables that she ended up. She thought to check on their horses, though there was little doubt that Sesa had been doing so. All the mounts were found in a corral with several others. Qala tried to recall the story Xido had told her of their escapade here, he and Marana and Saj, when they had lifted Flawum's crown jewel. They had stolen horses to escape, hadn't they, from a corral such as this?

The trio had practiced patience, made their plan, and succeeded. She must do the same.

136

40

"If Zedos grew up in the realm of the gods, might he not become as us?" asked Mawa.

Lenco considered the question. "There is no way of telling. Ha, I wonder if he might be able to change form."

"Not so long as he remains here and lives as a mortal," replied his sister.

"Then I pray he remains in this world," said Qala. She did not want her son turning into a crocodile or any other creature.

"We speak but of theory, my lady," spoke Lenco. "The two of us argue such things a great deal. Mawa, especially, likes to delve into what makes us as we are."

"Being half a god," said Mawa, "the lad might not even be fully tethered here."

"I must disagree on that point," came Lenco's response. "Not only was Zedos born in this world, and therefor attached to it, but he was conceived here while his father was fully human."

"Then he will always be a man?" If that were so, Qala was relieved to hear it."

"Not necessarily," stated the goddess. "He may be bound to this world but if that connection were removed, there is no telling what powers your son might achieve."

"He would have to come through a gate," Lenco pointed out. His sister only nodded thoughtfully.

Reluctant to do so, perhaps not really wanting to know but thinking she should have as much knowledge of her son and his relatives as possible, Qala whispered, "Gate?"

"Permanent ways between the worlds. They exist here and there, some easier to pass than others."

"Easier for us than mortals," added Mawa. "But if you were to find the correct pathway, you could come live with us."

"We could show her."

"But we would have to become somewhat human, first."

Lenco nodded. "Yes, to enter from this end. Of course," he went on, addressing Qala now, "as soon as we got home we would be our old monstrous selves."

"I prefer godlike," sniffed Mawa.

"I am not sure there is a difference."

"Please, not another debate," begged Qala. "Is there wine left?" Of a sudden, she thought of something. "Does the wine you drink here pop back to this world eventually? I would think that rather upsetting!"

Mawa brought the jug over and refilled her goblet. "That is not a problem for us." She turned to her brother. "Have we ever investigated the reason for that?"

"It has to do with us being connected elsewhere, rather than the other way around. Or something like that."

"Oh, right. Our bodies become gates of a sort."

Lenco nodded. "And so our shit stays where we leave it instead of popping off somewhere else, too."

"It would be handy if Zedos's did that when he filled his wrapping cloth," observed Qala, taking a quaff of her ruby-tinted wine. This was better than what she had imbibed before in the Pretender's keep. But then, they were not in the keep — Lingo the southern trader had taken a room in an inn, where he could come and go with fewer eyes upon him.

"Corad is supposed to be working on Lady Hasala" she continued. "His heart isn't in the work."

"He does not like the lady?" asked Mawa.

"On the contrary, he likes her too well. It is hard for him to deceive her." Both gods gave knowing nods. "None the less, we will find a way to get to my son's room."

"And when you do, I shall have the changeling ready," promised Mawa.

"I won't ask where you are going to get it, my dear sister," Lenco said. "Nor what it might truly be."

"That is wise," she replied. "I am returning home. Farewell, my Qala. May we have some more time to spend together some other day." She smiled a bit wickedly. "Or night." Qala chose to look away as she passed back into her own world. It was too disconcerting.

Lenco regarded his companion for a time before speaking. "Be wary of our Mawa and her webs. Oh, yes, you know this, but I say it anyway. We are all dangerous, in our ways, but she the most." He leaned forward, his eyes meeting Qala's. "Yet be wary even more of any of our family you have not encountered. They are not so fond of mankind."

"And you are, Lenco?"

"It is in my nature. So much so that it can be a distraction." Did sadness tinge his smile? "But I am not cunning like Xido, working his intrigues, seeing things beyond the sight of the rest of us."

"I know I was incidental to his quest for the Eyes. We all were."

"Do not assume things are so simple with my brother! You would not have had a child with him if they were. We were all perplexed by it."

"It couldn't be just, um, accidental?" It bothered Qala more than a little to think her son was but a part of a larger plan.

"Not with Xido. I suppose not with any of us." Lenco rose, facing her. "You are desirable, Lady Qala, and that part of me that is so fond of humanity desires you, as I have no doubt did Xido. But as a god of passion, of desire, I would not use that to further any plot. It is enough in itself."

"At least for tonight," agreed Qala.

41

"Flawum and, I assume, most of those here, know that we are friendly."

Corad nodded. "But they still believe we first met here."

"True," admitted Ranwif, "yet we rode in on the same day. That could raise suspicions."

"Too late to do anything about it," Qala pointed out. "But best we not be seen together with too much frequency, especially outside our rooms."

Corad's eyes went to her. That he wanted to ask questions about rooms and why she had not been in theirs last night was obvious. He worried, no doubt, she thought. But Corad would say nothing.

Yet she could not resist teasing him. "I left the room to you last night, Domos," she said. "I hope you used it to further your suit with Lady Hasala."

Ranwif stifled a snicker. Corad glowered but made no comment.

Sesa did. "You should treat this man with more respect," she scolded. "He has come all this way purely from friendship and loyalty!"

Perhaps no one was more surprised than Corad, for her sharp tongue had wounded him as frequently as any of them. "'Tis no great matter, Mistress Sesa," he mumbled. "But as to the lady, I think all I need do is pay her some attention. Flawum keeps her at arm's length."

"That is because he loves her," said Sesa, "and thinks he can never have her."

Corad nodded. "Exactly, my girl. He thinks it is his duty to marry this Vasema." He laughed ruefully. "And I think I have the same duty!"

Ranwif was somewhat incredulous of their assessment but stopped short of open scoffing. What he did say was, "But you believe the Lady Vasema dead."

"I did. I've heard too many conflicting stories here. This fish is dreadful, is it not?" He dropped the gummy fillet back onto his dish. "I ate better during my three years at the oars." He winked at Qala.

"I always thought we fed you rowers too well. It's ocean fish, that I can tell. Probably dried and brought back by soaking." She did not think much of it either.

"If only we had thought to bring Lovi with us!"

"I'd settle for Mistress Fee," remarked Ranwif. "Or even my own cooking, for that matter."

Qala said, "I think we could all agree with that. Our trip here proved you were the only who knew anything of cookery." The others nodded their agreement.

"Ah, my friend Benaro is far better. He'd make a grand cook."

"If I let him live," said the Mur. "That is still undecided." But of course she was not going to do anything to the boy. Maybe kick him off the estate, but not if he in fact did know his way around a kitchen.

"He's probably talked Domi into marrying him while we were gone," Sesa told them. It was hard to say exactly what Ranwif thought of that idea but he didn't look quite happy about it.

Anyway, they had more important things to ponder. "We must coordinate this within the next couple days," stated Qala. "I say this to all of you, if we don't carry through with this by then, I will go to Flawum and tell him all." She avoided looking at Sesa but the girl would know what she meant. "If you would wish to head north first, Corad, I will give you time."

He nodded his agreement. "We shall not all meet like this again. One to one communication from here out." He looked to the Muram woman. "And Qala makes any final decisions. Agreed?"

None objected. "Then let us finish this excuse for a lunch and go our ways." Corad paused briefly. "My way must be to the Lady Hasala."

"Ideally," said Qala, picking up from this, "the lady could give us access to Flawum's rooms while he was elsewhere, holding court or engaged in some duty."

Corad continued the thought. "Failing that, I might distract her — and perhaps the Pretender as well — while Qala went about breaking into the apartment and retrieving her child."

All assumed she would have supernatural helpers in that effort but none asked for details.

Qala could see Sesa was troubled. She might be thinking of going to Flawum herself, to save them from having to attempt this. But who was to say Zedos would be returned? She must wait and let them try this plan.

Would it be so bad for the girl to marry Ri Flawum, though? He did not seem a bad man. He had weaknesses, he was a bit foolish, he had no hope of ever regaining Sharsh, but he was a king of sorts. That trumped Corad, a future thegn — albeit a rather wealthy and influential one. Sesa had not shown any preference that Qala had noticed. Mostly a bit of disdain for both men!

For better and worse, there was a plan now and things were in motion. They must play out as they will.

42.

"I will not ask you for a comparison," said Mawa. "Though I do not remember anyone who had been with both in an exceptionally long time."

"Neither compares to you, my lady," answered Qala. The goddess would have to decide how seriously she meant it. Qala wasn't quite sure herself.

"Maybe I should seduce this Pretender for you," Mawa went on. "I could certainly keep his attention for a while. Even better if I could get Corad and Hasala to join in!"

This was turn around, to be sure, and definitely not serious. She chose to tell herself it wasn't, anyway. Qala decided to take things a different direction. "Though it is no concern of mine, I do rather hope that Hasala and Flawum get together."

"I've been working on that for some time," came a third and unexpected voice.

"Not the blond," moaned Mawa.

"Hello, Spider," said Esefa. "Eaten any husbands lately?"

"Better than having them cheat on me."

For a brief moment, Qala wondered whether Xido and Lenco had wives back in their world. She had never thought of that before — best she didn't now, either.

The Sharshite goddess ignored the jibe, and addressed Qala. "I've been working on your case too, but we have another reason to be interested in you and that is your son. Belore — my step-son, you know, but we get along well enough — does the prophecy thing and he thinks your little Zedos and his descendants are going to be pretty important in what goes on in Sharsh for a while."

Lenco did say her son's birth was no accident, didn't he? She chose not to delve into that right then. "I've seen statues of Belore. He's a handsome fellow if they are to be believed."

"Oh, he is. All the girls love Belore but Belore doesn't really like girls. Maybe if they're young and boyish. Ha, ha, my dear, I think you could almost be his type."

"I'm not so young." But admittedly a tad boyish. "He is not my type either." She glanced toward the other goddess in the room. "Maybe he should be introduced to Mawa."

"We know each other," was all Mawa the Spider had to say, and Esefa seemed no more eager to discuss the subject.

"What it comes to," said the fair goddess, "is that we are all working toward more or less the same goal — getting the baby home safely. If I can help get the pairings properly sorted out here, that's all to the better!"

"I apologize if Corad is getting in the way of your plans for Hasala."

Esefa laughed. It could be considered a musical laugh, depending on ones definition of music. "I suspect he is helping there. It could be the nudge she and Flawum need."

"Our schemes may be only little wheels, turning in some greater plan. But as long as we are after the same things now, it doesn't matter much." Mawa shook her head. "Further along, who can say?"

Esefa shot a suspicious look her way. "You know I am an open scroll, Mawa. When I love and when I hate, all can see it."

"And I weave a web of secrets. Yes, this is true. It is who we are."

The two had stepped closer together during this conversation, now standing nearly side by side. Esefa towered over the other goddess, her golden presence seeming to dwarf Mawa. Qala was not fooled into thinking she was the more powerful of the pair.

"Is it truly who we are?" Esefa asked. "I think we can change every bit as much as mortals do."

"I am not sure they can," was Mawa's dismissive reply, followed by sudden laughter. "You sound like Lenco!"

"The Snake can be wise." Esefa turned to Qala. "I am unlikely to interfere in the schemes at play here, either to help or to hinder, but I am paying attention. Many of us are." She pulled facets of light about herself, dazzling, almost blinding, as she exited the world of men. The room faded back to the dim illumination of one oil lamp burning on the table.

"I shouldn't be surprised," said Mawa, shrugging. "These Sharshites are her people."

"Where do your people live?" asked Qala. "I would guess to the south."

"Oh, we were the ancient gods of those now called Baxac. Many of them have forgotten us, save in their folktales." Mawa reflected momentarily, perhaps remembering those long ago times. "It is nice to have worshipers. It keeps us connected to things outside our world."

"But you do not need them?"

"It does not seem so. Something else Lenco and I sometimes debate. He says without our link to mortals we would be nothing but monsters." Mawa's expression hovered between a grimace and a smile. "Maybe we are."

"That may be true of we who are mortal too. I have known monsters among men." That she had. "I have known the monster within myself."

"And I have seen that which is of a god in you. In all humans. Monster and god in each of us, and who is to say which will have its victory at the last?"

43.

"My sister promises to be waiting to supply the changeling as soon as we reach Flawum's chambers."

"Still I do not like this plan," complained Budo. "Too complicated! Why could we not just grab my nephew and run?"

"Because Qala and her friends need time to get away," explained Lenco. Again.

Said Qala, "If any of my friends do run with me. It might be best if they remain and cover for me a day or two."

"Not too long," Lenco warned. "There is no telling how long the replacement child will stay put in this world."

"That also I do not like. It is unwise to bring whatever Mawa brings to this world."

Lenco appeared to agree with his half-brother's fears but did not speak to them. "I am known and shall walk openly with Qala to the doors of Flawum's apartment. From there — who can say what must be done?"

"And I meet you there," said Budo, "but do not show myself unless needed. Soon?"

"Now," replied Qala and turned to the door.

They did not mind being seen but, at the same time, there was no need to call attention to themselves. It was chilly inside the Pretender's pile of stones so they could wrap themselves up, hide their identities from a casual glance. Best no one remembered seeing them outside Flawum's door.

Left down the hall and then right to the main staircase, broad and much used. These were stairs of gray stone, part of the basic structure of the place. At the bottom, the ground floor, the audience chamber, the offices of functionaries, lay one way, the kitchens and the storerooms beyond them, the other. Qala and Lenco headed neither direction but turned back the direction they had come, into a long wide corridor. The guardsmen loitering along the way barely heeded them.

"So explain to me how we get in if the doors are locked," spoke Qala. The god had promised this.

"Most of our power," he said, "is akin to what sorcerers of your own world possess — the ability to change things in one world by reaching into others. I can send part of my being on a roundabout way and unlock that door for us."

"Is that difficult?" It would be a most useful ability!

"It is rather easy, at least for us. Budo can do it without thinking, just as he is able to move between our worlds and pull shadow about himself."

Qala thought of the Lady Esefa. She must work the same sort of magic. But instead of drawing shadow to hide herself, she chose dazzling sunlight. That might have to do with the sort of world from which she came, eh?

"Any of this does require effort and it can be tiring, but physically transporting ourselves is the most difficult." Lenco decided that was not exactly right. "No, not more difficult, just more work. That's why I don't simply pop into the room to open the door.

"Of course, Xido wouldn't have been able to do that when he completely took on man-form. He would have used the method I described." Lenco added, "Even your mortal friend Saj could have learned such tricks, with his wizardly abilities, and to speak to others from afar."

"I never saw Xido do any of this. He was quite lazy."

Lenco chuckled good-naturedly. "Perhaps so, my lady. He prides himself on doing nothing unless it is absolutely needed. Ah, here we are."

"With any luck, Corad has the lady-in-waiting and any of her attendants out of here," said Qala. "She often lingers in Flawum's chambers until he returns." She tried the door. Unlocked.

Left that way or had Lenco already undone the latch? No point in asking. Her companion knew the layout here better than she.

"Flawum's sleeping chamber is over there," he whispered as they slipped into the entry space. A servant could be heard in one of the other rooms, singing to herself. "The baby is in there."

This Qala remembered from her one visit. "I'll bring in just a little shadow around us," said Lenco, "in case someone enters." The Mur was at first surprised that it did not obscure her own vision of her surroundings in the least. Well, of course, thought Qala. It is no different from standing in a shadowed place and looking into one that is lit.

Lenco, however, did seem a bit hazy when she glanced toward him.

And then she was with her boy. No nurse about? Oh, dozing in a chair, her knitting in her lap. Best they did not awaken her! She carefully lifted Zedos. It was good to have him in her arms again.

Mawa made no attempt at softening her entry and, without warning, Qala wasn't able to look away from the chaos of images quite as quickly as she might have wished. The goddess held a small bundle in her arms, seemingly identical to the one in her own.

"In the crib," whispered Lenco, "and we'll be out of here."

Qala glimpsed the changeling as Mawa slipped it into its bed and pulled the covers around the little form. It wouldn't fool her but others might not notice the differences.

One child began to squall — which Qala was not sure — and then the other took it up. The nurse stirred and, opening her eyes, saw the intruders gathered about her little charge. Not surprisingly, she screamed.

Then her eyes widened even further and she screamed again.

44.

Flawum did not like to begin his audiences early but took his time before going about any official duty. It was past mid-morning when he entered the room and took a place upon the throne.

Sesa and Ranwif had been waiting for some time. If the Pretender tired of his audiences, or if he wound up the day's business, it was for them to attempt to delay a return to his rooms. It was to be hoped Flawum would have no reason to hurry back.

In other rooms, not far from the royal apartment, Corad should be making tryst with the Lady Hasala. That made it sound somewhat clandestine, didn't it? An innocent lunch with the lady, that was all it would be, keeping her distracted while Zedos was kidnapped for a second time. How exactly that abduction was going to be accomplished was something of a mystery to Ranwif; he would leave it up Qala and those friendly gods of hers.

Flawum seemed to be stepping a bit gingerly as he entered, favoring one foot. Maybe the gout was acting up again. As he took his place on the throne, a servant brought a stool and pillow so he might prop up the aching appendage. To the right of the throne — really naught but a high-backed wooden chair with some so-so carving — rested the sacred stone on which Sharshite kings had traditionally been crowned and atop it, on another pillow of yellow silk, lay the royal crown. Ranwif knew the golden-hewed jewel set into that crown was only glass. The Earth Stone, one of the Eyes of the Wind, had been stolen from it nearly two years ago.

Many times had Ranwif stood in this audience chamber, the throne room of the Ri, but it was still new to Sesa. She had been in here briefly when first they arrived. "What do you say?" he whispered to her. "Would you want to live here?" He hoped for a 'no' but the girl only shrugged, giving no answer.

Men and women came and went, presenting petitions, speaking on behalf of this or of that. Visitors were presented, and requests for safe passage of the realm. It was shaping up to be a long and tedious session; Ranwif was willing to endure that if it gave his friends the opportunity to act. He wondered how Corad's more pleasant assignment was going.

An aide came and whispered in the ear of the man who claimed to be Ri of Sharsh. He nodded, turned to his chief minister and made a slight, barely noticeable gesture of the hand. The man rose and announced an immediate end to the audience for the day.

A moment later, Flawum also rose and strode — as best he could with his sore foot — toward the double door. Ranwif felt it best to follow. The Pretender was in conference with a handful of men in the hall, men who had the appearance of just having ridden hard.

He slipped outside, Sesa remaining unobtrusive behind him. As long as Flawum was busy with this group, he need do nothing. But it was too soon for the Pretender to be heading back to his own chambers.

There were lowered heads, nodded heads. Voices murmured, not loud enough for Ranwif to hear. Then Flawum spied him and waved him over. "These men have just returned from the north," he announced, "where they were delivering our request for the return of my intended bride. The young woman there insisted they had no such person on the estate, nor that she had any idea where she might be." Flawum turned back to the men. "She was not the mistress of the place, was she?"

"No, my liege," said one. "The woman claimed the lady of the manor was traveling and had left her in charge. She had some disreputable but capable-looking men at arms to back her up, so we chose not to press."

"The lady was traveling even though her son was taken?" Flawum shook his head in bewilderment. "I wonder again if you took the wrong child!"

At that moment, one of them looked up, glimpsing Sesa. "My lord," he exclaimed, "this is the woman we almost had!"

His comrades turned to stare at her, and one corroborated the identification. "Aye, your majesty, that is Lady Vasema. How came she here?"

The Pretender was truly confused now. "This willful girl is Vasema?" Flawum did not seem at all pleased with the idea. Then another thought occurred to him. "That fellow who rode in when you did, Ranwif — is he who he says he is?" Confusion turned to concern turned to alarm. "He is with Hasala!"

Giving no orders, the man turned and hurried toward his apartments. The others followed, leaving Sesa and Ranwif standing there in the hallway.

"It appears Flawum won't take the time to arrest anyone right now," remarked Ranwif. "Should we make a run for it?"

"And desert our friends?" asked his companion. "Never."

"It is quite possible they have succeeded and are riding north themselves," he reminded her.

"And if I ran, men would be sent after us immediately now my identity is known. If I remain, Flawum may not care about the others. But you could go."

"I am not one to desert either, Sesa." Ranwif laughed and shook his head. "We might as well return to our room and wait."

"After lunch," she replied. "I've worked up something of an appetite."

45.

There was another making an entrance, not easily as did the gods, but laboriously pushing its way through to another world. A misshapen head could be glimpsed, and tusks, amid the shifting images.

The nurse sprang to the crib and grabbed up the changeling. "I'll keep you safe, little one!" Her eyes darted here and there, wildly, uncomprehending.

A banging of the door, the stamp of many feet, as Flawum and his men burst in. "We heard a scream," spoke the Pretender, gazing upon the confusion within the chamber.

Qala had just enough Sharshic to follow what had been said. "I have thrown shadow around us," whispered Lenco to her. "We could try to slip out but it may not be possible with all this turmoil."

"What is it?"

"A mafadwi. A monster from my world," the god told her. "And the mother of the changeling, if I am not mistaken."

Mawa remained visible, her slender body standing between them and this monster. "She can not match the mafadwi in that form," said her brother.

"Then I will stop it," declared Budo, taking form beside them. He again held his heavy club. The massive god shook his head. "Stupid Mawa!"

"I agree," spoke Lenco. "I shall try to get Qala and her son out of here." The men who had entered were ranged around the door now, uncertain, staring at what was going on. It would be impossible to slip through them. "We must wait."

Qala only held her boy tightly and remained quiet. But she longed to be able to have her knife in her hand, to stand and fight whatever threat she and Zedos faced.

The mafadwi now was completely in the room. She was tall, taller than the bulky Budo, and long of arm and leg. Short, heavy tusks sprouted from the lower jaw, curving up toward surprisingly large eyes, and both fingers and toes ended in claws. The lean, muscular body was naked and hairless — and was that a tail Qala glimpsed, restlessly waving back and forth?

"Mong!" she shouted, her voice like the wind through a deep chasm. Both babies cried loudly at the sound. The mafadwi looked about, confused by this.

Budo stepped forward, brandishing his cudgel. "Do not make trouble here, Ir!"

Mawa glanced at her half-brother, standing at her side, protecting her, though he had little reason. "You know this monster?"

He answered not, but Ir, the mafadwi, did, glaring at the goddess. "You took my Mong!"

"I was only borrowing him for a little while," claimed Mawa. "You know he would have popped back."

"Want him now!" The mother mafadwi's eyes went back and forth, resting first on the cringing nurse and then going to Qala.

"She can see us," the Mur whispered.

"So it seems," was Lenco's only answer.

The monster stepped forward. Budo's club swung, only a warning. "Go back, Ir," he told her. "I'll fix things."

"No. Give Mong now!" She fixed her great golden eyes on Mawa. "Or I eat sister."

"Do not make the Spider come forth," warned the goddess, "or you will be one who is eaten."

The mafadwi was not going to be reasoned with. Qala could see that; would she be any different, placed in the same situation? Why didn't they just let her take her little one, now their plan had gone so awry?

Budo apparently had the same thought. Not as dense as his siblings thought, was he? "Take him and leave," he ordered. "But hurt no one here!"

"I didn't know a mafadwi could cross worlds," whispered Lenco,

153

musing only to himself, perhaps. "She must have followed the bonds that connected her son to his home."

Ir stepped forward slowly, cautiously, showing she meant no harm, while Budo kept a watch on her. Mawa had backed away now, clearly exasperated by the way her plans had played out. The mafadwi stared at the nurse, huddled on the floor, protecting as best she could the child she held. "Mama," spoke Ir, nodding her head, and turned away.

"Mong!" She leaped toward Qala, her long arms reaching. Too late did Lenco try to get between them; far too late did Budo even realize what was happening. And Qala's strength could not begin to match that of the mafadwi. Zedos was taken from her arms and Ir disappeared in a cloud of disorienting images.

Seconds later, Mawa did the same.

"We must hide," said Budo. "Shadows, brother." He and Lenco held the distraught Qala, too shocked to make any sound.

Flawum came forward, staring at the empty space where he had lately beheld monsters, monsters such as he would never have believed existed. It is notable that the Pretender was the one with the courage to do so; he was not so useless as many thought him. He knelt by the whimpering nurse.

"Were there two babies? I thought I saw two." Flawum picked up the changeling and peered at it. "This — does not look like the same child as before." The little being growled at him. "It doesn't even look human!"

There came a sudden sound like a great wind. There was a flaw in the air, a broken place, opening like a ravenous mouth, ready to devour. The changeling child was pulled into it and Flawum the Pretender went with him.

Part IV.
A NEXUS OF KIN

46.

"The mafadwi must have weakened the forces that held her child here when she opened a way for herself, don't you think?"

"It could be so," agreed Budo. "But I do not care."

"And so it shot back to our world sooner than expected. Poor Flawum with it!" Lenco was amused by this. Qala was not.

The trio had ducked into a darkened side-passage not far from the Pretender's rooms. "We must go after them. Now."

Both gods agreed. "Shall I take her?" asked Lenco. "Or do you think maybe a gate, instead?"

"No time for that," replied his half-brother.

Lenco turned to Qala and informed her, "Budo is the most knowledgeable of us when it comes to gates. He is somewhat our unofficial custodian of them."

"Just get me there somehow. Oh!" She remembered some of what she had been told before. "Won't Zedos pop back here on his own?"

"There is no telling how soon," said Lenco. "We need to get him away from that mafadwi."

Budo said, "I don't think Ir would hurt him. And now her own little boy should be back with her." The burly god did not sound quite so sure as his words suggested. "Also —" He sounded reluctant to say what else was on his mind. "The boy is half a god. He might not be drawn back to this mortal land."

"This is true," Lenco admitted. "He might be as we are. Anyway, we have to go rescue poor old Flawum, if your friend hasn't already eaten him."

"Also," said Budo, "to help Mawa. She chased after them."

Qala had wondered about that. "Then you will take me, Budo?"

"I shall. Let me gather my strength a moment. It is not so easy to take someone with me."

Lenco nodded. "Then I travel with you, since I know not where Ir dwells. It is too late to follow in her wake."

Budo turned to the Muram woman. "It is not hard for us to move between the worlds but you are tethered here, so it takes more energy to carry you along. And it will not be permanent — sooner or later you would be pulled back."

"To the same spot, right?"

"Oh, yes, exactly the place you left," answered Lenco. "Right here in this dingy hall. If all goes well, we'll bring you back before anything like that occurs. Coming back will be easy, like floating downstream."

"Close your eyes before we go," Budo warned. "There are things you should not see."

Lenco chuckled. "'Tis bad enough we have to see them. Ready?"

"Yes." Qala did shut her eyes tightly and kept them closed. The trip did not seem so bad, but it was as if a strong wind had been blowing against them. She felt the ground grow solid again beneath her feet, and caught the scent of flowers. There were the cries of birds, too.

"We are here," announced Budo.

"The valley of Krat?" she heard Lenco ask, as she opened her eyes. "I knew not anyone dwelt here."

It was a valley, a deep jungled valley, vast blue mountains rising ahead, brilliant greens and reds and golds about them. "It is the ancient home of your father," continued Lenco. "We have not seen him in eons."

"Our father," Budo corrected him. "Krat always treated you as his own. Ir has taken residence in one of the caves."

"I do not approve." Qala had not heard such anger in the god's voice before. "Mafadwi do not belong here."

Budo shrugged. "Then you throw her out." A slow smile came to his face. "And her friends. It is ahead." The god turned and began walking along a stone-lined path.

Had the sky ever seemed so brilliant a blue before? wondered Qala. The leaves so many shifting shades of green, the flowers quite so red, quite so fragrant? Was this how it was in the worlds where gods lived?

She would grow tired of it, she thought, as she and Lenco followed. Budo turned toward a tall, narrow fissure in the red-brown cliff wall they had paralleled. "Here. Be ready and be careful!"

Inside was not the dark sandstone of the cliff, but a cave of crystal, rising in glittering arcs above, to disappear into a thick darkness. A fire's light illuminated the depth before them. Against it a slender feminine figure stood in silhouette, surely that of Mawa.

A group of figures beyond, still not readily made out in the flickering ruddy light. Qala found herself noting, of all things, the cleanliness and order of the place. Not what she might have expected of the cave of a monster!

And there squatted Ir, flanked by two other monsters, both female mafadwi. Flawum sat nearby, looking none too happy. Two babies nursed at the mafadwi's breasts.

47.

One of Ir's companions had two heads and dead-white skin but otherwise seemed relatively human. The other looked more a great lizard than a woman; the greenish tinge only accentuated this.

"Those are their only shapes, their true shapes," whispered Lenco in Qala's ear. "Mafadwi do not shift as do we gods."

Ir peered at Qala and then down at one of the infants she held.

"Is god-child," Ir stated. "Yours?" Her eyes focused on Qala.

"Yes, my Lady Ir."

"Xido is the father," Budo volunteered.

"Like Xido. Sorry I get mad at you, Budo."

"You had good reason," the god admitted.

"Budo is our friend," said the lizard-like monster. "Unlike some." She gazed balefully at Mawa, as did all four eyes of her companion.

"I have apologized," spoke the goddess, maybe just a little too haughtily. "What else can I do?"

Ir laughed raucously. "Many things, Spider! But I think we give boy back. Good boy. What is name?"

"Zedos," answered Qala. "I thank you for taking care of him."

The monster woman nodded amiably and turned her eyes to Flawum. "Maybe I keep man and have fun with him? Demdem and Nerua too."

Her companions seemed to like that idea. "Eat him later!" said greenish Nerua.

"Only after we tire him out," added Demdem. Her other head agreed.

"No eating," decreed Ir, obviously the alpha female here. "He special man!" The mafadwi looked at him with a hunger that had nothing to do with her stomach.

The Pretender looked up at her and then turned to his would-be rescuers, giving them a resigned shrug. "Aside from the tusks, she is not so bad looking." Qala had to admit that was so. "I don't mind the tail either," he said, as an afterthought.

"He belongs to another world," spoke Lenco, stepping forward. "You know he will be drawn back to it. Every part of him."

"Not so sure, Snake." Ir leered at her Sharshite captive. "More to him!"

Nerua asked, "How else Mong bring him along?"

"I was wondering that myself," admitted Mawa. "But he has none of our blood." All eyes went to Flawum.

He had nothing to offer but confusion. "I don't understand any of this. I don't even know where I am!"

"With new wives!" one of Temtem's heads informed him.

Lenco gave a firm shake of his head. "You know we can't let you keep him."

"You take him, little Lenco?" snickered Ir. "Maybe I keep you in cave too, eh?" Her sister mafadwi eagerly nodded in agreement to the idea.

Mawa's voice rose, clear and commanding, the voice of a goddess. "This is my responsibility," she said. "Take the baby and leave. I shall deal with it."

Both her brothers seemed hesitant about this but Qala was not hesitant at all about taking her son when Ir held him out to her. "Go!" Mawa ordered.

Budo turned and took Qala's arm. "This is best. Come with me." He started toward the cave's entrance, a sliver of blue in the dark.

Lenco was more reluctant. "Very well," he said, after staring at the tableau before him for a few seconds. "We leave it to you, my sister."

In short order, they were stumbling out into the near-blinding sunlight in the valley of Krat. "Will Mawa be alright?" asked Qala. In her mind, she saw that slender form being torn apart by the monsters she had chosen to face.

Lenco's laugh held little mirth. "I only hope she doesn't slaughter all three of them."

"Our sister the Spider is powerful," came Budo's steady voice. "Fear not for her."

"In part," spoke Lenco, "she too is a mafadwi, a monster. We all are."

Budo nodded. "Our ancestors."

"Yes, we are descended from them but perhaps not only from them. Some say the gods arose from the mating of a mafadwi and a human. Or maybe something that looked human."

"The gods of our world," Budo corrected him. "Who knows the origins of other gods in other realms?"

"Indeed so, my brother. It is possible that a god from one of those other worlds is involved in our evolution, one of the most ancient, perhaps."

"There are humans here, then?" asked Qala.

"We keep some to serve us but it is a dangerous world for them."

"This is true," said Budo. "The mafadwi do not mind eating them at all!"

48.

They followed their jungle path in silence for a few minutes before Lenco chose to speak again. "We should tell you that Mawa isn't entirely trustworthy with humans either." He sounded rather reluctant to impart this information.

"She might want to keep this Flawum herself," added Budo.

Qala thought on this, but not very long. "I wish the man no harm but it is not my concern. I have my son and that is enough. When do we go back?"

Neither god seemed willing to give her an answer. "There are things we must sort out," Lenco said at last. "And we all need to rest, even if it won't be so difficult returning." But he was eying the child.

"Be honest," spoke Budo. "It will be easy to take you back, my lady, but we are not certain about Zedos. He is partly of this place."

"And he nursed at Ir's breast," Lenco mused. "Who knows what might result of that?" He shrugged and went on. "Anyway, we really should get Flawum back. It is our fault he is here."

Qala was slightly surprised that the god felt an obligation. She had not been sure he had any morals at all.

"It is not so far to Mawa's home," said Budo. "We shall go there and await her." His tone suggested there was no other choice. "But we need not walk all the way. There are —"

His explanation, if that was what was coming, was interrupted by a sudden shimmering of the golden light before them, as Esefa stepped into their world. She looked about her. "Much as I remember," the goddess remarked, and turned toward the four. "I have come because of the royal Sharshite that got pulled over here. He really should be put back where he belongs."

"It is likely that Mawa has him," said Budo.

"Ah, do you think she will behave? No, don't bother to answer that. I am not staying nor shall I attempt to assist if problems arise," Esefa stated. She seemed quite firm on the subject. "I could not hope to match the Spider's power in her own home. I am uncomfortable with even being here for a few seconds."

"Then why have you come?" wondered Lenco.

"There are things you should know. For one, Flawum just happens to have a little divine blood from a few generations back. It might manifest itself here." A slight smile came and went. "His family boasts of the legend though I doubt they truly believe it."

"Your husband?"

"No, I can not blame Jov for this one. An uncle of his raped the woman. Or we think it was so; as some of your relatives, they are little better than beasts. Great ugly giants, most of them." Esefa grimaced at the thought of her in-laws.

Lenco nodded, for her words had brought comprehension. "This was what made him attractive as a mate to Ir," he said, "and why she thought he might not be drawn back to his life."

"I would think so," agreed the goddess. "If he needs to be guided through a gate — assuming you can rescue him — I'll come and assist. I'd be interested to see if he develops any godly power." She turned to Budo. "I suppose you would be the one to get him back."

"Most likely, Lady Esefa," he agreed.

"Then let it be as it will be." The daylight shattered and the goddess left them.

"As I was saying," spoke Budo, "we need not walk. The gods have shorter paths."

"What my brother means is that gates exist within our world. Permanent passages between different locations. One lies nearby." Lenco added, more softly. "My father was last seen entering it."

"You can't just move around like when you come to my world?" asked Qala.

"Not permanently," Budo replied. "And it is exhausting."

"We sometimes do it when we simply have to be with someone immediately. This way is much better," Lenco assured her. "To you it will seem as a great cavern, with many tunnels leading in and out."

"And maybe it is," said Budo. "Here is the way."

It appeared yet another cave entrance. "Hold onto one of us or you may be unable to pass in," Lenco told her. "And we'd best be touching little Zedos, as well. No telling how the guardians will react to him."

They entered in something of a clump, both gods with an arm about the Mur, each with a hand on the baby. Qala could feel nothing but she saw the brothers give each other knowing nods. Then they were inside. A cavern indeed! Huge it was, its vault disappearing into an unmeasured vastness. All about were passages, the mouths of caves, leading — somewhere. This she could feel.

"This one," spoke Budo, and they plunged into its blackness.

And stepped at once back into light. A silvery light, in a place replete with shadow, it was. Before them, by a dark stream flowing languidly through forest, lay a rather ordinary house, with a thatched roof above a post and beam construction. Qala had seen such in her voyages south, on islands in the steamy tropical seas. "Mawa's home," announced Budo.

"I had expected something, um, grander," was all Qala could say. It was not exactly small but it was certainly not what she had envisioned as the abode of a goddess.

"No bigger than she needs," replied Lenco. "After all, we have no one to impress save ourselves. Let's see if my sister is home yet."

49

The house proved empty, even of servants. Did Mawa leave it un-locked, unguarded? wondered Qala. Or did these brothers of hers know their way past any obstructions?

Zedos had become fussy. "My son needs food," she told them. "Maybe not right away but not too long either."

Lenco did not seem happy about this. "The less he eats here, the bet-ter. We want to avoid tying him to this world."

"But we can not let him starve, Brother," Budo reminded him. "The milk of the palms can sustain him for now."

"That might not hurt," conceded the god. "I shall bring some."

"Good," said Budo the Boar as he left. "I am too big to go climbing palm trees."

Whether Zedos actually liked what Lenco brought him can not be said, but they did manage to get some of the milk into him. Then all three adults, god and mortal alike, collapsed onto woven sleeping mats. The baby did not awaken them through the night, but it may be they were too tired to hear him.

There was other food in that house of Mawa, so they were able to breakfast the next morning, some food that Qala recognized, some that she didn't. Weren't the gods reputed to consume some unique and magical nourishment? This all seemed ordinary enough, and a bit starchy.

It was past sunrise when they spied a worn and bewildered Flawum accompanying Mawa toward her house. The goddess seemed wrapped in her own thoughts, doing little more than acknowledging her guests' presence before disappearing into a chamber.

"Tired," was Budo's assessment.

"I do not know why she would be tired," protested her mortal com-panion. "I'm the one who did all the work!"

Eyes turned to him, asking questions. "I had to please those — ladies," Flawum explained. "They demanded that I, um, service them before I could leave and your friend agreed to this. But not until after she changed into a most huge and dreadful spider and threatened them!" He shook at the memory. Or memories. "So I spent one night as the price of freedom."

"I wish Mawa had not allowed that," muttered Lenco, "nor permitted herself to change form. But it is done."

"I was glad to see that she had turned back to a pretty girl when she came to collect me in the morning! It was not so bad a night. I can't remember ever having so much energy. I say, there must be something in the air here!" The man did not seem embarrassed by his adventure; perhaps he was even pleased with himself.

"Undoubtedly," remarked Lenco. Once again he and his brother exchanged one of those meaningful looks. What the meaning was, Qala had no idea but doubted it was good.

"We should inform Mawa of what Esefa told us," spoke Budo.

"Esefa?" asked Flawum. "The goddess? I would like to meet a deity!"

The brothers but laughed. "Come," said Qala. "There is food and a place to sleep. I think you could use both! And you," she said turning to the gods, "get some more milk for Zedos."

Lenco bowed deeply. "At your command, my lady." But before going, he warned Budo, "Keep an eye on our sister. I like not her mood."

"Nor I," agreed his brother.

The thoroughly confused Pretender stuffed himself on the unfamiliar breakfast items — it was a race between whether he would first be sated or fall asleep from weariness. "Who are those fellows?" he asked, between mouthfuls. "I recognize Lingo but not the other one."

"They are those gods you said you might like to meet, gods of the Baxac people in the south. And the Spider is their sister."

"Oh. I was afraid of something like that. I've been sent to the wrong afterlife, haven't I?"

Qala might have laughed if the weariness and worry of the past days had not worn so heavily on her. She but smiled weakly and told him,

"Not dead, sir, only transported by accident to their realm. We are all going to get back to where we belong."

"That would be good," he agreed, "but the only place I am going at the moment is to sleep." He did not awaken until evening.

Nor did Mawa show herself much until late in the day, slipping out a couple times to gaze into the distance and barely noting her guests. Qala and the gods spent much of the day sitting on the veranda of her home, tending Zedos as needed but mostly just resting. That house lay on a low rise by the river, the dark river with its overhanging trees. All the valley seemed a place of shadow, the mountains closing it in, a se-cret place and a place of secrets.

"Are your homes like this?" Qala asked her companions.

"Built the same," replied Lenco, "but in a much brighter location. I love the warmth of the sun upon me." He pointed a thumb toward his brother. "Budo chooses to dwell in a cave like a mafadwi."

"There are worse places," came Budo's amiable response. "And the roof never leaks."

50.

"I think Mawa is having trouble maintaining her form," whispered Lenco.

"It's the mortal's fault," came Budo's reply, whispered as well.

"Me?" asked Qala.

"No, Flawum," Budo said. "She wants him."

His brother nodded. "Being around those mafadwi may have caused this. The Spider is taking over. We can not permit this."

"Would it be so bad?" Qala wondered. "More pleasant, I would think, than those three monsters who had their way with him." She had definitely enjoyed her own encounter with Mawa.

Lenco raised an eyebrow. "Pleasant? Maybe, but Mawa has a bad habit of eating her mates when she is done with them. It's just her nature."

"Instinct," Budo told her. "She becomes mindless. Mawa could do other harm while she is that way." He turned back to his brother. "We should warn her of Flawum's heritage."

"She must sense it. That might be part of what drives her."

"Oh, yes. Maybe so." The big god frowned. "It would not be good if he gave her a child. Dangerous!"

"It would be bad enough if he got one of those mafadwi pregnant," felt Lenco. "You'll keep an eye on them, won't you?"

Budo did not answer but turned his head toward the doorway. "Someone is up," he reported, before turning back to his companions.

"Most of all," Lenco continued, "I would worry about our nephew. We know part of Mawa wants to keep him here as her own. That part may be ascendant if she becomes the Spider."

More sounds arose from the interior of Mawa's house, not loud. Budo, of a sudden, asked, "Does that sound like eight feet to you, Brother?"

Lenco strained to hear. "No, not now, anyway. It could have been for a few seconds." He sighed. "We must deal with her." He thought on that for only a moment before deciding, "I must deal with her. You must get the mortals away safely."

"I understand," stated Budo. "All is quiet again. It would be best if we did not have to do this in the dark." The sun was already disappearing behind the steep slopes.

They sat for some minutes, each with his or her own thoughts. Lenco stood. "A light," he murmured and reached out. An oil lamp appeared in his hand, borrowed from some other world. "We can eat, at least, and make our plans. With luck, we will not have to act before dawn."

They entered Mawa's central hall, seeing no sign of the house's other two residents. It was a tall room; all the chambers in this house seemed spacious, far more so than needed, thought Qala. "I'll bring some food," she offered. "If you want anything cooked, you are on your own."

"There are servants about to take care of that," Budo informed her. "They have not shown themselves to us but they are here."

Qala was surprised to find several cooked dishes waiting in the next room, bowls of pasty substances she could not identify, fruit, fish. "Come," she called. "There is too much for me to carry." No answer came.

Holding Zedos in one arm, she returned to her comrades, finding them standing and attentive to something. What? "That way," said Budo, and started off, Lenco behind. Qala saw no reason not to follow — better than being left alone with those hidden servants!

"In here," spoke Budo. There were no doors to the rooms, only cloths curtaining some of the entrances. He brushed one aside, as the three pushed into the space. Oh, thought Qala, as her eyes became used to the faint light, it's Mawa and Flawum. Her instinct was to make a quick and embarrassed exit, and leave the pair to their business.

Not the two gods. "She is not holding to her form," said Lenco. It was true. At moments, Mawa seemed the slim dark goddess she had

168

known; at others she seemed something larger and of a shape not at all human, with many legs. Qala was not sure the goddess' lover was aware of this.

But Mawa was aware of them. She shouted something, but it was not coherent and ended sounding more like a hiss. She rose from the side of Flawum and — the woman was no more.

A great black spider, not the shiny, bulbous sort that hangs in webs, but a shaggy hunter stood before them. Big as a horse she was, no bigger than that! No wonder Mawa needed spacious rooms. Her eyes, four jewels of aquamarine, glittered at them, swept from one to another, until they rested on Zedos. "Run!" shouted Lenco but Qala was already on the move. The Spider leaped forward, no longer concerned with her lover, the instinctive urge to have the boy for her own all that drove her.

Budo slipped by his sister and grabbed Flawum — who was once again completely bewildered by what was happening around him — and threw the naked man over his shoulder. Knowing the walls were but flimsy hanging mats, he burst through one with his burden.

Qala had paused in the hall, uncertain of her next action. She would not blindly blunder out into the jungle night! "Come," yelled Budo, as he reached her. He set the Pretender down. "We all run! It is up to Lenco to stop the Spider."

Before turning to flee, Qala glimpsed the slight god backing into the hall, the great arachnid creeping after him. Then — did he too change? She had no time to see but was running, running as fast as she might and hanging onto her son, following Budo. She assumed the Pretender was running with them but he was not her concern; let him keep up if he could!

The moon had arisen, astoundingly bright. Qala looked up. No, not the moon but two moons stood in the sky. The three runners stopped for a moment, catching their breath, regrouping, and looked back toward the house of Mawa. There before it rose a great serpent, the color of jade and reticulated with deep gold, holding the dark shadow of a spider at bay. Then they were running again.

Back to the passageway through which they had reached this place she assumed. And where from there?

The opening appeared before them, a darker shadow in the shadow of a cliff. As before, Budo made sure to hold onto all three mortals, lest one somehow fail to pass through. Then they stood again in the great cavern.

"We go to my home," was all Budo said, and led them toward one of the passages.

51.

"How could I turn down the chance to make love to a goddess?" asked Flawum. Qala had no good answer for that. She might well have done the same. She *had* done the same.

They had emerged from the tunnel in a quite different part of this world. The moons were still above but now their light fell on a rocky terrain, high up in a mountain range. Tall conifers stood in the valley below them, nearly as black as the night itself.

Budo had brought them up a steep pathway to a ledge that looked out over immeasurable distances. "My home has a view," he said, and led them into a roomy cave. Little magics, such as must come natural to these gods, soon had lamps and a fire lit. It was rather nice, thought Qala.

The god looked at Zedos. "I have nothing to feed the child," he apologized.

"I am told he is of an age to begin on solid food but it would not do to start him all at once," said Qala. "I don't think." She was still uncertain about child-care in general.

Budo seemed more knowledgeable. "No, it would not, but a little might not hurt." Then, more to himself than anyone else, he said, "I wonder if I could find a nurse."

"Another of those monsters?" asked Flawum, flopping down on a pile of straw that apparently served as furniture. He looked up at Budo and asked a rather shrewd question. "Or are you gods pretty much monsters too?"

"In some ways," said Budo, "and in some ways not. As with men."

"Very true," said the Pretender. "The, um, spider can't follow us here, can it?"

"Mawa shouldn't be able to get through the gates in her present form. Of course, she could run the distance on those eight long legs in a couple days without using any shortcut. She will know where you are." He changed that. "She will *sense* where you are. I'm not sure she knows anything much as the Spider. It is a very mindless, very primitive form that Mawa takes."

He paused before adding, "More so than any of the rest of us. Are you hungry? I always keep a full larder."

Budo did not lie. Soon a feast was spread for them, nothing fresh, mind you, but all good food, and a quite decent beer to wash it down. "A spoonful or two of my brew, maybe mixed with water, should not hurt Zedos at all," Budo felt. "It is the beer of the gods, after all." The child certainly didn't seem to object to it.

After, they rested before the fire, welcome in these chill heights where lay Budo's cave. "There is no telling how long Lenco and Mawa will remain in those shapes," the god told them. "Maybe not long, here in our own world."

"Should we wait for them?" asked Qala.

"I do not know. They are smarter than me, this I *do* know, this they know. I would like their counsel before trying to send you home."

"Lord Budo," spoke Flawum, "I understand little of who you and your siblings are. Gods — very well. That is simple enough. But what are these other forms? Do you have one as well?"

"I do," said Budo, answering the last question. "I am the Boar. And as such, I have the most brains when I change my shape!" He laughed. "Pigs are smart."

Smarter than spiders, thought Qala. Or snakes or even crocodiles. But surely there were other gods in this world she had not met. Lenco had warned of them.

"When we were young," Budo continued, "we were as the mafadwi, but as we grew we learned to shape ourselves, divide our two natures, monster and god. The two exist in different worlds but always connected."

He turned his eyes toward Zedos. "The boy sleeps. That is good." Qala's child did seem healthy and content, despite all he had been through, despite the irregular feeding of the last two days. "I think

172

maybe," the god continued, "the milk of Ir nourishes him still. It is potent stuff for a human child."

"I'm feeling pretty well nourished myself," remarked Flawum, yawning. "And I now I need a great deal of sleep. And maybe some clothes." The man had been carried from the house of Mawa without a stitch and now sat wrapped in a ragged blanket he had found in the cave.

"My kilts would be too large for you," Budo told him, "and no others live here. I keep no servants, human or otherwise."

"Then this must do. Where can I lie down?"

"Where you are. Or anywhere else you choose in the home of Budo." The god turned to Qala. "You may use my bedchamber," he said, pointing to a curtained area deeper in the cavern. I will watch here."

He settled himself at the entrance of the cave, and turned his eyes to the night.

52.

"Xonxon knows of a nursing female," said Budo. Qala had arisen to find her companions in conversation with a horned mafadwi, a male. "He could bring her."

"Are we going to stay that long?" she asked. Qala wanted to be home, and soon.

Flawum felt the same. "It would be nice to be on our way," he said.

"We wait," stated Budo and gave no further explanation. "Bring her," he told Xonxon, who hurried from the cave. "A mortal woman, not a mafadwi," said the god. "Best I clear that up, eh?"

"As long as Zedos is fed, it matters not."

Budo nodded. "I need advice on all of this. I know not what to do! I would even listen to Xido right now." He sighed. "But he is a beast, too."

The cave seemed lighter for a moment, as though the sunlight finding its way through its entry had grown stronger. "Perhaps we could figure something out," spoke Esefa. "But I too would welcome the thoughts of your clever siblings."

"I welcome you, my lady," said Budo, "and your counsel. Oh, Flawum, you said you would like to meet the Lady Esefa."

The man seemed too astonished to answer. Apparently Esefa was his idea of what a real goddess looked like, tall, regal, golden. "M-my lady," at last he gasped out.

She gave him a gracious nod. "I am not sure I know any better course of action than you, Lord Budo," admitted Esefa.

The god did not seem surprised. "The safest way to get all of them back would be through a gate. Then there is no longer a tie between them and the world they leave. You understand," he said, turning to Qala, "that you are not entirely here in this world. Part of you remained behind, so that you exist in two worlds at once."

"We gods can control this, when it comes to our own bodies," added the Sharshite goddess, "but not yours. Sooner or later you will be pulled back."

Budo took up the explanation again. "I fear if we just took Zedos home the way he came, he might pop back here unexpectedly. Maybe Flawum as well. Their beings have become entangled in both worlds and it is hard to say which will pull them hardest. You, my lady, should not present any problem. But of course you would want to accompany your boy on his passage to your world."

"Of course," echoed Esefa. "Any mother would." She surveyed the group. "I think you all need rest today. No need to make a decision now — at worst, one of you might be pulled home." Her eyes went to Qala. "If that happens to you, my lady, we shall certainly get your son to you as quickly as we can."

"And if either of the other goes, we will know they are not tethered to this world and there is one problem less. So yes," agreed Budo, "we wait today and regain our strength."

"Then there is no need of me here," spoke Esefa. She stood looking at Flawum for some time, assessing him, perhaps. "There have been changes in you, Ri of Sharsh, but I know not how great. We may not find out until you are again home." She reached out her arms, pulling sunlight to her, and disappeared into its prisms. Flawum was fascinated; for the other two, familiarity bred, well, familiarity.

It was a day of rest all appreciated, once they had it. Some time passed before the mafadwi Xonxon returned with a reluctant woman, her own babe on her hip. Qala was not particularly surprised that the human resembled the gods, physically, but could see no actual reason she should.

But she did nurse Zedos, who seemed entirely willing to suckle, though apparently not very hungry. Alas, the woman spoke a language of which Qala could make no sense, nor answer when she appeared to ask questions. "She wanted to know if the child is a god," Budo informed her. "It made her happy to be told it was."

Qala now wondered why this woman of Budo's world could not

communicate with her but the mafadwi could. It must be a god thing was all she could decide. She would as soon leave such riddles behind her and have Zedos safely home.

"And serving the gods might be enough reward for her," Budo went on, "but I should gift her in some way for this." He rummaged about in one of several large iron-bound trunks that lined the rock walls. "Ah." He pulled out quite a sizable ruby and gave it to the woman. "Jewels such as these mean little to us here. What would we do with them?" he asked. "But mortals enjoy the baubles."

He spoke to the returned mafadwi. "Escort her home, Xonxon, will you? My thanks for your service. And say hello to your mom." Budo turned back to Qala. "I make an effort to get along with the mafadwi. They can be useful." He closed the trunk. "You don't care much for baubles, do you, Lady Qala?"

"Only for what they can buy, Budo."

He smiled at little Zedos. "You now have things baubles could never buy."

"But I would not have my estate without them. I would have no place to raise my son."

"A boy needs more than an estate," Budo said, and began to turn away, before returning his gaze to her face. "As do you, my lady."

Qala laughed, trying to sound dismissive but knowing she failed. "Do any of us get all we need?"

Budo smiled in return, his big homely face wistful, saying, "But we try, Qala."

There were no more words as she took his hand, walking beside him to his private bedchamber.

53.

"She was still the Spider when I left," reported Lenco. "Mawa resists relinquishing the form." The god had found his way to his brother's cave during the night.

"It can have a strong hold," Budo said.

"All the more reason to get our guests back home," Lenco stated. "I think you are right about the gates being the best way. I — do sense connections, especially with Flawum. We need to break those."

"I've mapped out a path," said Budo. "Let me tell you of it." The two went aside and huddled, Lenco for the most part nodding agreement with Budo's plan.

When they rose from their conference, Lenco announced, "Budo knows these ways best. We shall follow his route. At once?" he asked his brother.

"Yes. There is no reason to further dawdle here. I may have you all home in time for supper!"

"That sounds fine, Lord Budo," said Flawum. He had taken to addressing these gods with considerable respect since his encounter with Mawa the Spider. "Um, sir," he asked Lenco, "you won't be turning into a snake again, will you?"

"Not unless it is needed and maybe not then."

"I thought you a most attractive snake," remarked Qala. "Quite a bit prettier than you are now."

"That's for sure," agreed Budo. "Now here's what will happen. We shall return to that cavern through which we passed before. The cavern may exist in all worlds in some form. Or between all worlds."

"Or maybe it doesn't exist at all," said Lenco, "and is but how we must visualize the rifts between realities."

"Maybe," agreed Budo. "But I am not our sister so I shall not argue the point."

"Or we would be here all day! The only thing that matters is that it will let us pass to other worlds. Some of those worlds — such as ours

— hold more gates than others. Some gates are easier to access than others. And we can not go directly through one to your world from here — at least not if we want to end up anywhere near where you left!"

"So it will be a roundabout journey," concluded Budo. "But it starts here and now." He led them from his cave and along the rocky path, descending toward their first destination.

"It should not be surprising that we place our homes nearby to these gateways," said Lenco as they walked. "It is so convenient."

"But maybe dangerous," was Budo's thought. "Anything might wander out of one."

"That is rare. Most who manage to enter at all become lost eternally. Only a few ever find any sort of way out, and then often into perilous worlds."

"Then we are fortunate to have competent guides!" spoke Flawum.

Qala's only comment was, "So they claim."

It had been dark when they had climbed this way. Now the steep canyon walls could be seen, the unbelievably high mountain peaks beyond. This was a world of excess! Everything higher, brighter, more beautiful, maybe more deadly. The viridian firs moaned in the winds that rose from an unseen depth, rushing upward among the crags.

"I say, isn't that Lady Esefa?" asked Flawum. The goddess lounged nonchalantly along the way, brushing bits of wind-borne debris from her blue gown. "Going to join us, you think?"

"I don't know why she would," muttered Lenco. "Maybe just wants to see us on our way."

"There you are," said Esefa as they neared. "I didn't see any reason to walk all the way down so I waited here." She looked the party over. "Guide them well," she said. "They are important."

Esefa fell in with the group as they continued to descend. "I hope to see you in your own world soon, Qala. You, Ri of Sharsh," she told Flawum, "will most likely not see me again. But be assured I shall have my eye on you." Then she drew close and whispered something in his ear. The man nodded thoughtfully, saying nothing.

"So you are not going with us, Lady Esefa?" asked Qala.

"No reason to, my mortal friend. Others can better show you the way."

"Perhaps, Qala," Budo blurted, seeming shy of a sudden, "if I showed you the way through the gates you could come back through them. Then you could live here without fear of being pulled away. Ze-dos, too. There is room for you both in my cave or — or anywhere else you wished."

Lenco smiled indulgently at his half-brother, but it was Esefa who spoke. "Zedos belongs to the world of his birth." She seemed quite adamant about this. "It would not be right to keep them here, Budo. Besides," she said, her voice softening, "you know Qala does not love you. I am working on finding her the right woman."

"And not Mawa!" said Lenco. "She might well have invited you too, if she wasn't being the Spider right now."

"Quiet!" growled Budo. "Something comes." He listened, turning his big head back and forth, hearing sounds none of the others could. "It is Mawa," he said. "The Spider."

"I'll be of no use here," declared Esefa, just a touch of fright entering her voice. She promptly opened a door and stepped through, not even bothering to hide it in light. The many facets of the goddess assembled and shattered and some did not all resemble a golden-haired woman.

But there was not time to ponder that! "We must reach the cavern before Mawa," shouted Lenco. "She can not enter in that form." But that was not to be.

She squatted near the door, her eight hairy legs spread out, ready to leap at any who tried to pass. "Can't we reason?" whispered Qala.

"No more than you could with the spider that spins by your own door at home. Only the mind of the spider is awake in her," said Lenco. "I must become the Snake again, though I fear it may be hard to leave behind this time."

"Nay, Brother," spoke Budo. "You lead our friends home. I shall deal with Mawa."

And he changed. Tall he grew, and fell onto four legs, with great forequarters roped with muscle. Stiff bristles rose from his back, tusks curved in his powerful jaws. He was, in essence, the greatest, most fearsome boar Qala had seen, as massive as — ah, she had never seen a beast so huge! He dwarfed the Spider, yet she leaped fearlessly toward him.

"Come," urged Lenco, hurrying the humans toward the opening in the rock. Behind them rose the sounds of battle.

54.

Then they could hear no more, all of a sudden. It is as if we entered another world, thought Qala, and maybe they did. The cavern was as before, seemingly endless, with innumerable passages opening from it.

"Will he be alright?" whispered the woman. She had grown fond of Budo; this was so.

"I do not know," admitted Lenco. "Her venom would not harm me, when I am Snake. When we were young, millennia ago, we would play at fighting each other in our beast forms, so I know this. This may not be so for Budo."

"I would that I could have fought," she said. Was she not once Queen of Pirates? Was not her steel the equal of any man's?

"And slay my sister, maybe? I know you would not wish this, Qala — let the gods deal with the gods. Now we must find our way through this maze."

"We have to visit other worlds along the way?" asked Flawum. "That is what it sounded like Lord Budo said."

"Yes, but we need not travel far through any. I am not sure some of them are truly worlds at all, only floating bits of being. Our longest walk will be a mile or so. But even a mile can bring dangers."

He seemed to be counting the cave mouths before them. "This one," he said, and led them in. Almost at once, they stepped out into a sunny meadow. "One of the trickier gates," murmured Lenco. "Invisible. Hmm, there." He stepped forward and disappeared. His companions followed, exceedingly quickly.

And they were again in the cavern. "First leg accomplished," proclaimed the god. "If we had time, it would have been a nice place to dawdle. Aside from the frolicking man-eating unicorns."

Qala was not sure whether to believe this. "Here," said Lenco, and led the way into another passage. They emerged in a moonlit valley. Only one moon here, she noted. "We have to cross this little rill," Lenco told them. "The gate is over there. Don't worry, this is a safe one." They waded the cold, shallow water and climbed the far bank, where Lenco again plunged into a cave opening.

"Naturally," he said when they were again in the cavern, "we use closely-placed gates where we can. The problem is, they get more traffic so increase the odds of running into hostile individuals of one sort or another."

"I wish I had my sword," spoke Flawum.

Mine too, Qala only thought, and then considered the Pretender. He might be well-schooled in weapons. Nobles generally were. Still, he was soft and lazy.

"The next is the long one," warned Lenco. "And it is rugged country." He took them to a desert landscape of sand and jagged rocks, a yellow sky above. "The gate is over that hill," he said pointing. "A temple was built around it by the folk who once lived here."

"They are gone, sir?" asked Flawum.

"Long ago. They all became insane one day and committed suicide. Why?" He laughed. "Because it could be. Anything that can be, will be, somewhere."

Qala remembered his discussion with Mawa, when first she met the god. "Didn't you once argue that things didn't exist until men discovered them?"

"That I did, my lady! I might even believe it on some days." They made their way through the wasteland. "Be careful of the scorpions," warned Lenco. "They are particularly pestilent here."

The ruins of a shrine could be seen ahead. Was that a statue of some strange beast before it? "Oh, a sphinx," groaned the god. "I haven't time for this."

"What is a sphinx?" wondered Flawum.

"That's right, they are not in your world nor your legends. Fortunate people, you are!" He paused for a moment. "Well, we must get by it." Lenco resumed walking toward the gate.

"Snake!" the creature greeted him. "A long time has it been!" Compared to the mafadwi of Lenco's world, Qala did not think it particular-ly fearsome. Pretty large though, the body of some sort of big cat, hu-man head. Human-looking, she decided; not actually human at all.

"This does not seem a profitable place to hang out," responded the god. "What do you here?" He did not address the beast by name. Qala suspected the god had forgotten it.

"The weather I like! Never rains. You pass through?"

"We do. And we pay no toll to you."

"I ask none. You would crush me in your coils if I insisted. But have you nothing for a poor mendicant in the desert?" It — no, she — eyed Zedos. "That looks tasty."

"Let me pose you a riddle, sphinx," Lenco replied. "What sort of creature gets in the way of a god and ends up dead?"

"A most stupid one, lord! Please pass." They entered among the bro-ken stones and descended a short stairway. At the bottom they again stood in the cavern.

"If I had the time I would have become the Snake and rid the infinite worlds of another pesky sphinx. But I suppose there are an infinite number of them, too." Lenco looked about. "Two more and we'll have you home. Close to home."

The next world was one of fire and liquid rock and noxious air. "To our left," shouted Lenco, and had them into another gate in ten min-utes with no harm. "Our last world contains the most dangerous crea-tures of all," he warned them with mock solemnity. "Men."

He found the appropriate tunnel, but paused at its entrance. "We should come out rather near your keep, Flawum," he said. "It was not entirely by accident that the Earth Stone ended up where it did."

"Earth Stone?" asked the Pretender.

"The one that used to be in your crown," Qala told him. "You didn't know its name?"

Flawum shook his head. "Hardly matters now, does it?" he chuckled. "Shall we go?"

55.

It was necessary to quiz some peasants as to their exact whereabouts. Flawum did this, as the man spoke far better Sharshic than Qala. It is to be noted that Lenco was also fluent in the tongue — perhaps in all tongues — but had deserted them almost as soon as they had reached their world. "I must get back to check on my sister and brother," he had said.

The god did not need to go back the way they had come, of course. He opened a door in his usual way and was off. Nor could Qala and Flawum detect the gate through which they had passed, seeing only a small, smooth hill before them. But they had come out of that mound in some fashion.

"I hope he lets us know how they are," said the Pretender. "Oh, I know he will tell you. Just pass it on if you can. But carefully! It wouldn't do to have you arrested for treason by the Muram Empire."

Yes, Lenco would undoubtedly visit one day, and maybe little Zedos's other relatives. Who might know, his father could even show up. It didn't matter much to Qala at the moment. She wasn't even sure she wanted to return with the Pretender to his keep. She could head north to her own home.

But that would be impractical with no money, no horse. Best to stay with the man and count on his gratitude. His friendship. The man who claimed to be Ri of Sharsh was a friend.

"I am sorry that I got you into all of this," she said. "Had I not harbored that girl —"

"I would not have had the first true adventure of my life," he said. "And what an adventure! I won't be able to convince anyone of what happened, you know."

"Hasala would believe you."

"Hasala, yes. But I'd best leave out some details, eh?" He became briefly introspective. "It will be good to see Hasala."

Having no other option, they were walking toward his still somewhat distant keep. Thoroughly disreputable they looked, particularly the Pretender, possessing naught but a worn blanket as his garment. Couldn't Lenco have reached somewhere and found them a little gold? wondered Qala. Ah well, she should have thought of that before he left them.

"Perhaps I can pass as a wandering holy man," suggested Flawum. "You could hold a bowl for the alms of passers-by."

"It would be easier to rob them," was her answer. And Qala was considering it. But, curiosity piqued, she asked, "What god would you serve?"

"I wouldn't be a Jevote. They're not liked in these parts. Maybe one of the old Ildin gods. Say, I wonder if they have a world of their own too? Now that would be interesting to visit, wouldn't it?"

"No," she said, and hoped it was the end of the conversation.

It was not. "If I were truly a priest," he went on, "I would serve Ese-fa. Isn't she wonderful?"

"I don't know. I haven't slept with her."

Qala was immediately afraid she might have offended the man but, no, he stifled a laugh. "I suppose that is as good a way to judge ones gods as any. I just missed out on that with Mawa."

"Oh, she is the best of them all," Qala told him. But in her heart she knew that would be sweet, solid Budo. If she could love a man, would that he were like the Boar. Even better would to be find a woman with his character! Ah, that was probably better than she could hope for, and better than she deserved. She had her son. Let that be enough.

They were near the keep before there was recognition — but not of Flawum. "It's the woman we were to watch for," a passing soldier told his comrade. "The Muram trader who disappeared."

"So it is. Who's this beggar with her?"

"This man has useful information about Ri Flawum," claimed Qala. "Best you get us to the keep immediately!" So it was they were marched into the castle and before the chief minister, who sat perusing papers at his ornate desk.

The man looked up, not recognizing the Pretender for a moment. "Your majesty!" He rose in astonishment. "How? Allow me —"

Flawum held up a hand. "Before anything else, have someone find milk for this baby. The same wet-nurse as before if she didn't flee the place. We shall be in my apartment." He turned to Qala. "Will you accompany me, my lady?"

"If there is food at the end of our journey, anywhere."

"And a good bath, too," he promised. "But Zedos first." He peered at the boy. "He looks surprisingly well." Flawum led the way into and down the hall.

"We've never quite straightened all that business out, have we?" he continued. "Now this is the boy my men kidnapped and is also your son. This I know." He squinted as he got things straight in his head. "And it was the correct boy and you are the mistress of that estate — what do you call it?"

"Melawhem."

"Oh, yes. I like the name. And you really were harboring my intended bride, who is actually the girl Sesa."

This statement surprised Qala. "I didn't know you had learned that."

"Only moments before I was whisked away while hanging onto that baby monster. So I assume Domos was working with you."

"Yes. A trusted friend. Ranwif too, of course. He felt rather responsible for all that had happened."

"Ah, here we are." They entered the Pretender's rooms, preceding the rumors of his return. Those were undoubtedly making their way through the entirety of the keep. "Bring us supper," Flawum ordered the first servant he encountered. "And draw two baths." He turned to Qala. "I keep two. One was my late wife's. And here is our nurse!" The woman took Zedos from his mother's arms and to the next room, mumbling something about monsters not getting him away from her this time.

"And your friends — your accomplices," he said, chuckling. "No harm will come to them. All forgotten! Indeed, I thank them and I thank you, Lady Qala. I have learned much and now must change much."

"I can see this, your highness. Even I who have known you for so short a time. Why even your limp is gone!"

"So it is, my lady. So it is."

56.

"We didn't know what to do, your highness, so we kept everything quiet, hoping you might, um, come back the same way you went." The chief minister smiled with some self-satisfaction. "And so you did, it seems!"

The man stood before them in a red caftan, embroidered with thread of gold, much of it broken and hanging in glittering filaments, where not missing entirely. Flawum looked up from the supper he was sharing with Qala. "I realize it seemed far longer to me than it truly was. Still, I am surprised no one missed me."

"I, um, told visitors that your gout was acting up, sir." He paused, and added to that, "Except Lady Hasala. I thought she should know the truth. We did not say anything about, um, Lady Vasema either." The minister eyed his master's companion, unsure whether to speak further on the subject with her present.

"Lady Qala knows all about that," the Pretender told him. "She was the one who harbored the girl." Qala herself seemed to be paying no attention, playing with the boy in her lap. But she was quite aware of all that transpired.

"Qala, is it?" The Sharshite raise an eyebrow but made no further comment on her identity. "Very well, sir, very well. None but I and my personal envoys —"

"Henchmen, you mean," said Qala, glancing up for a moment to the Sharshite and then back to her son. "We know what to call them, don't we, Zedos?" Though she chose to speak in Muram the men recognized that she could follow their Sharshic exchanges.

And so the minister replied in the Muram tongue, "As you will, my lady. I know you encountered them under unpleasant circumstances."

"And slew two of them," she reminded him.

"Um, yes. At any rate, they are most discreet and mentioned nothing." He regarded the Muram woman for a few seconds. "We did not discover you were missing for some time, as well. Your husband was greatly troubled by this."

"Not her husband, not that it matters," Flawum informed him. "What did you do with the man?"

"He and our other, um, guests were confined to their rooms until we sorted things out. We had no real reason to be suspicious of this Domos, but felt it a wise precaution."

Qala snickered. "It's good that you kept him out of trouble." She might be making a jest of it but she was quite serious. Corad could have blundered in all sorts of ways, given his freedom.

"So whom should we call first to us?" wondered Flawum. "Or just get a good night's sleep and attend to everything in the morning?"

"If everyone knows we're back, there would be no hurry," felt Qala. "And I know we both need rest. Might I stay here the night, my lord, with my son and his nurse?"

"Absolutely, Qala. You need never leave if you do not wish it! Ha, I shall appoint you my personal bodyguard." It was possible that he was, in part, serious. To his chief minister, Flawum said, "You may go. Do make sure that my return is known to Hasala, will you?"

"Yes, your highness," said the man and exited in the formal manner, stepping backward, bowing, and then turning to the exit. There would have been seven steps back in the throne room but space did not permit that here.

Whose room was this? wondered Qala, when shown to her bed-chamber. The late queen's? Or would she have had a separate apartment when she needed space between her and her husband? Not important; exhausted, she fell into sleep at once.

Yet it did not last. In the night, sometime, Qala awoke and and could sleep no longer. After a time, she got up and lit an oil lamp of carved stone from the banked fire in the hearth. This is Hasala's room, isn't it? she thought of a sudden. Where she sleeps when she need tend to the man she loves.

In a darkened corner, shadows shifted, coalesced, and two figures stepped forth. Lenco. Mawa — ah, but her arm! The goddess' left arm was missing.

Mawa could see her shock. "It will grow back," she quietly informed her. "One of my legs was broken off in the fight." She gazed at the floor. "And then I ran home and curled up and became — me, again."

"I returned too late to see the end of their battle. Only a certain amount of blood and ichor, and Mawa's missing limb were there to give evidence of it," reported her brother. "I climbed the way to check on Budo. Swollen, he was, from her venomous bites, but our brother is not badly injured. It takes a great deal to kill a god!"

"For which I am thankful," murmured Mawa. "Though to whom I should be thankful, I have no idea."

"To Budo, maybe," said Qala. Both gods nodded an agreement.

Mawa spoke further. "I can remember the things I did, not as thoughts but as pictures. As if watching someone else. Ah, I am sorry. My wants grew great and became my needs. They may still be my wants but the hunger of the Spider no longer drives me."

"For that too we must be thankful," said Lenco. "We must be back to our world but thought to tell you how things have gone there. And have things gone well here, Lady Qala?"

"So far," she answered. "But tomorrow has not yet dawned."

57

"I do not believe I need to see your friend Domos," announced the Pretender. "But the other two, yes." How will he choose to deal with them? Qala asked herself. Would he claim his bride? Would Ranwif face punishment? He had assured her otherwise but when kings change their minds, none question it.

"Have them brought," he told his minister. "Lady Hasala, as well." He turned to Qala. "You can tell Domos yourself that he is free to accompany you home. When you are ready, my lady. I shall not shoo you out of my home!" He helped himself to another fried cake. Flawum had consumed more than she felt wise, already.

"I only need to arrange a few things, sir. Most importantly, how to feed Zedos on the way home."

He waved a hand to dismiss this difficulty. "We can provide a nurse and a wagon. Or a cow! Whatever you need, Lady Qala."

He looked toward the door. "Are they on their way? Oh, of course, mind me not. You," he said, addressing his chief minister, "must be ready for changes here. Yes, many changes." Flawum nodded rather vigorously. "Ah, here we are."

He rose. "Lady Hasala, welcome. I am pleased to behold you this wonderful morning. I thought I might never again! Hmm, let's wait for the others. Have a seat, my dear."

The perplexed noblewoman settled into a chair by the wall. Vasema and Ranwif were ushered in shortly after. "Ah, young Ranwif. You first," spoke Flawum. "Oh, you have all breakfasted, have you not? Good. Now as to what I should do with you." He considered the youthful Sharshite as if weighing many options. This, Qala was fairly sure, was a sham.

"You chose loyalty to your mistress," said the Pretender, nodding toward Qala, "over loyalty to your king. Which do you choose now, lad?"

"I must correct you, your highness. I chose loyalty to the Lady Vasema."

"Ah, so that is way it is. Then, Master Ranwif, I turn you over to her to do with as she will." He smiled with genuine warmth. "You are welcome here as a friend but I no longer count you among my men."

He never was, Qala could have told him. She did not.

"Now as to the lady. Come forward, my girl." Vasema strode forth stoically, like a prisoner facing sentence. "It seems you ran from both husbands who had been chosen for you."

"I would be free to make my own choices," she announced. The quaver in her voice kept her from sounding quite as brave or defiant as she might have wished.

"Ah, so 'tis about freedom, not love. Well, I shall make no claim on you, my lady, but if you wish not to go to this, ah, what's his name?"

"Corad," two or three voices informed him.

"Yes, Corad. If you wish, you may remain here and choose whatever man you choose! Ranwif, even."

She looked at the boy and shrugged. "Anything is possible, your highness."

"Indeed it is! I like you, my girl, but I think I would fear to marry you. Which turns me to my next order of business this morning. Lady Hasala," he said, standing and facing the lady-in-waiting who had, indeed, been waiting a long time. "Will you marry me and be my queen?"

Flawum held up a hand to silence his minister when it appeared he was going to raise some objection. "A goddess whispered to me that this would be," he said. "Who am I to question that?"

"Not I, my lord," answered Hasala. "Indeed shall I marry you."

"Good. Then that is settled. Should have been long ago!" He turned to the rather dazed-appearing chief minister. "Arrange the wedding for, mmm, the Yule. A new beginning for a new year. Is that acceptable to you, my dear?"

Hasala nodded an assent. She looked nearly as dazed as Flawum's minister.

"One more item this morning. It is a wonderful morning, isn't it?" There were confused murmurs, mostly agreeing with the Pretender's sentiment. "Not something that concerns all of you but as long as you are here, you will be my audience!"

He returned to his chair and picked over the remaining cakes, before turning all of them down. "Cold," he told himself. "Now," he said, raising his eyes to those in the room, "it is time we recognize the foolishness of going on as we have here. We are no kingdom, just refugees in a patch of wilderness, with the mountains on one hand and the coastal swamps on the other, not worth the trouble of rooting out.

"Not yet. Someday the empire will decide to put an end to us, and it will. We all know this. I will never rule all of Sharsh."

"But your highness —" began the chief minister.

"But what? Am I wrong?" The man had no answer.

"I propose to approach the Mura. Make some sort of peace with them. If necessary, renounce my title. It would be best for all."

Silence greeted his words. It was Qala who finally said, "It would improve trade, that's for sure."

"You understand, my lady," he said, inclining his head to her. "If I bring peace and trade, then I have truly served my people."

58.

The trip north was slow, even tedious, compared to their dash south. This must be, for they traveled this time with little Zedos and his nurse.

Now they were vulnerable, riding openly. That was no problem the first few days; a guard of the Pretender's equesters accompanied them. In time, they would pass out of his protection and into lands occupied by the Mura. There was that lawless frontier between; there lay the most danger.

Corad no longer made an attempt to disguise his identity. Nor did he disguise his interest in young Sesa, who often rode beside him. Yes, as Sesa he knew her, still completely ignorant of her identity. Qala had ordered all to keep him that way.

When Sesa rode not with Corad, it was with Ranwif. Qala had no quarrel with either man paying the girl court. Let her decide on either or neither. If she wished instead to continue to be Sesa, to work at Melawhem, Qala would welcome her presence.

And perhaps Ranwif had forgotten his idea of marrying the Muram woman. She had never taken it seriously. Not really. Let others find love now. Perhaps she would tomorrow.

Sometimes she rode her pony, holding her son, beside the nurse. A cart had proven unnecessary — this was not the nurse who had tended him in the keep of Flawum but a younger woman, a slight girl named Samee, who thought maybe Melawhem would be as good a place as any for her and her own baby girl. It was an Ildin name, Samee, and many of that heritage lived in the south.

As to whom the father of her little one might be, Qala did not ask. But they spoke much of other things, giving both Qala a chance to improve her Sharshic and the girl one to begin learning Muram.

"Is it a great estate?" wondered Samee.

"Melawhem is — mmm, of somewhat middling size, I suppose. Lord Corad's father is master of far greater properties than I." She nodded in the man's direction, where he rode before them.

"He likes Sesa," observed the young woman and, judging as only a pretty girl might, added, "She is not much to look on."

"You will learn, my girl, that matters amazingly little in the end."

In time, Flawum's horsemen left them, and the lessened party continued on their way. It seemed wise to avoid the eyes of men, any men, and so they did.

Or so they attempted, until they rode about a bend and found themselves facing a mounted Muram troop. "Best make ourselves known," spoke Corad, riding forward, his hand held up in greeting. "I am Lord Corad of Sarowhem," he announced to their leader.

The man eyed him, perhaps with some suspicion, but answered, "We've been told to keep an eye out for you, sir." He looked over the rest of the group. "It was said you were on a rescue mission in the south."

"Indeed, so, Captain," said Qala, bringing her horse up to stand beside the Sharshite's. "He delivered my son from the keep of the Pretender!"

"Oh." Did the man look disappointed? "The word was you sought a young woman. A local noble of some sort."

"The Lady Vasema," Corad informed him. "I believe she has perished."

"Hmm. Would that I had the time to hear your tale! But you should be safe enough riding on north and we must continue our patrol. Strange reports have been coming of the Pretender's court." His dark eyes swept their party once more. "Maybe you are part of them but that is not my business. Fare you well, travelers." He and his soldiers, all Muram lancers, rode on, their polished cuirasses flashing in the sunlight long after the men themselves could no longer be made out.

That sunlight was growing weaker, day by day, as winter came to these lands. It was as when Qala had first come, a year before. And, as a year before, she arrived at her estate. It was now grown familiar, and so different from the world in which she lived once.

"Before we ride in," spoke Corad, halting the group. "I wish to share my news with you. There may be too much going on an hour from now!" His gaze went to Lady Vasema and his gaze held — what, love? Or perhaps only fondness and admiration. Qala could not be sure.

"Flawum will not be the only one to wed on the Yule," he continued. "I have asked Sesa to be my bride and she has agreed. This my parents must accept on my return." The nobleman seemed thoroughly certain of this.

"Oh, how wonderful!" whispered Samee. "She will be a great lady!"

"So she will," agreed Qala. She watched Ranwif but he showed no emotion, one way or another.

But before they rode into her manor, Vasema brought her horse close and spoke to Qala. "I shall do my duty after all," she laughed. "He is a good man and we like each other. That he was willing to go against his parents and marry an unknown peasant girl was enough to decide me."

"He thinks you would make the sort of partner he needs. I think he is right."

"Yes, you have been letting this happen, haven't you? Who knows how different it might have gone had he known my identity?"

"You will tell him soon?"

"Maybe." Vasema laughed again and spurred forward to ride by her husband-to-be as they entered Melawhem.

59.

"I knew you would come back. All of you. Zedos!" Domi held out her arms and received the baby. "Oh, and another child!"

"Samee, this is Domi." Qala thought only for a second before adding, "My bailiff."

"Mistress Domi," said the girl, curtsying. It was likely no one had ever curtsied to Domi before.

As to what any of the others thought of the unprecedented appointment of a female bailiff, we can only guess, for much else swept those thoughts away. "Your father's men have been pesterin' us," Domi complained to Corad. She would not, of course, say 'our father' in public. "The crew has been backin' me up."

The three former pirates were ranged behind, attempting to look like reputable men at arms. "And Benaro. He helped a lot."

Qala fixed her eye on the young farmer. "We must deal with you," she stated. "Inside. Let's not all stand out here."

They repaired to her hall. "Food, Fee," called Qala. "We have traveled far and missed your cooking!"

"At once, my lady! It's good to have you back." The stout cook disappeared into her kitchen and Qala turned to Benaro. She had wondered from time to time of how to deal with him on her return, and something Ranwif said had given her an idea.

"Here is my sentence on you, young man. You will leave my estate." Benaro appeared crestfallen but resigned. "But only for one year. That year will be spent, Lord Hurrum agreeing, in the kitchens of Sarowhem, learning from their cook."

"My father will agree," spoke Corad. "I shall see to that." He turned to Ranwif. "And you, sir, I offer a chance to train as one of my equesters. No, you need say nothing now. Only consider it."

"I don't need to consider my sentence," spoke up Benaro. "I will study with Master Lovi."

Ranwif studied Domi for a moment before saying, "Yes, my lord. I will consider it."

Augun was at the door. "Mistress," said he, "the envoy from Lord Hurrum wants to speak to you. Him and his men have been bothering us for days!"

"Send him in," she ordered. The man, one of Hurrum's equesters, was plainly surprised to see Corad.

"Your return will be pleasant news to bear to your father," he said. "And perhaps it can help us clear up all this mess about the missing noblewoman."

"That is to be hoped," remarked Corad. "Are her parents at Sarowhem?"

"That they are sir, and most upset about all this. Reports — no more than rumors, your father thinks — came that news of this Vasema was kept secret by Lady Qala. Her parents demand that the lady be brought before a judge for impeding the search. The Lord Vullum is insistent on this. Or his wife, the Lady Galana, I should say, and he does as she says. She is most distraught by the disappearance of her daughter, I think, and wishes to blame someone."

Corad seemed to dismiss the whole affair. "My father is magistrate in this district. He would certainly find in your favor," he told the Muram woman.

Qala decided to play along with this for the time, even knowing it would come to nothing. "But his is not a Muram court. Remember that I am a citizen of the empire and can not be judged by a Sharshite, no matter how noble."

"Could not this be waived?"

"It would set a bad precedent. I must retain my status in the eyes of my neighbors." It wouldn't hurt for those neighbors to be aware of this.

"Very well, my lady. It is an attitude I quite understand." Corad grew sober. "I do dread facing Lady Vasema's parents with no good news."

"Who is to say?" asked Qala. "There might be word of the lady yet."

"But I most definitely shall not wed her! I have chosen Sesa and that is that."

"We shall all ride to your home on the morn," said Qala, "and sort things out. Now, let us eat!"

It was good to be back in her own chambers that night, her son safely in his cradle. Resting in fact, next to Samee's own child. As the girl had no family here, she might as well reside in Qala's apartment. It would be handy.

And Domi and Sesa back together in their room, if only for the one night. The two were likely to talk until dawn. Soon to be sisters-in-law, too.

All was well and with any luck, no more adventures would intrude on her life. Peace from now on was Qala's wish; peace with none of the restlessness and bouts of despair she had known in her old life.

One candle yet burned in her bedchamber. In a moment, she would extinguish it, too, and search through the darkness for sleep. But the light in the room grew greater then, not less.

"Lady Esefa," she greeted her visitor. What a time to come, with her so weary!

"So," began the goddess, without indulging in any pleasantries, "Corad and Vasema. You helped me with my work there, Qala."

"It was just a matter of getting out of the way."

"Indeed. It is a good match, like many others, and of no great significance. Other than love always being significant."

"Do they love?" wondered Qala.

Esefa laughed. "Corad does. Vasema is willing to tolerate his love."

"Maybe he'll grow on her."

"It is likely. I expect happiness for Hasala and Flawum as well. Even if his mind wanders to other worlds now and again." The goddess grew pensive for a moment. "Unknown parts of the man have been awakened. But let us speak of you, my lady!"

"I think I've had enough attention from the gods," she stated.

THE CROCODILE'S SON

"Ha, maybe so, but I promised you love and I am working on it. You'll meet Lady Galana tomorrow. You might like her — she's been known to dabble." A slight and sad smile hovered on Esefa's lips. "But that's not love, of course."

"Even without meeting the woman, it sounds like a bad idea."

"Maybe so. I would like her to find love someday but it might be beyond any god to grant that. Not so for you. I know you can love, Qala, for once you did."

"Yes," agreed she who was Queen of Pirates. "I did."

60.

A messenger had been dispatched to Sarowhem nearly as soon as the travelers returned. Now some of those travelers followed the same road.

Who rode? Corad did, and the woman he had sworn to marry, Sesa-who-was-Vasema. With them went Qala, and the men of Hurrum. No others. Let the young people sort themselves out at Melawhem. Benaro could come when he was ready, Ranwif if he decided.

"I understand this Lord Vullum is quite under the thumb of his wife," remarked Corad. "A nonentity, married to an heiress. Not even very good-looking!"

"And I understand he is quite a handsome man," objected Sesa. "It is said his daughter resembles him."

"With that mother, this is surprising."

A seething Sesa said nothing. She can wait, thought Qala. She will have her chance to bring Corad to heel.

The River Chas lay blue-gray and cold beside them, the trees along the way now mostly without leaf, rising in colorless forests or naked among the dun fields. They passed between the markers of Sarowhem's boundaries without comment.

But the girl was checking out everything. This was to be her realm and a competent ruler she would be.

To the doors of Sarowhem they rode, where Lady Belema and Lord Hurrum waited. It had not been so long — far less than the three years he had been captive! — but they greeted him as one long lost. Perhaps having once lost him, they would ever do so.

Corad's parents gazed with some curiosity at his companions. Qala they knew, but not why she was there. As to the girl, they had no idea. They might even have thought her the Mur's maid.

Corad pulled her forward, right there in the courtyard. "This is Mistress Sesa," he announced. "I am going to marry her."

Perhaps it was best to say it at the first opportunity!

"But — she is not noble, is she?" asked Belema.

"It matters not," replied her son. "She will be my wife."

Hurrum frowned. "Best we discuss this inside." He gave Sesa an up-and-down look and shrugged. "And best you not speak of this to the Lady Vasema's parents. It might seem an insult so soon after their loss."

A tall woman appeared as they entered the thegn's great hall. "There she is! Are you going to arrest her?" A harried-looking thin fellow was close behind her. Both glared at Qala.

"I do not think that is necessary," came an even, quiet voice. Vasema stepped forward.

"Sesa!" roared her father, rushing forward and embracing her. "We so feared! We so feared!" Lady Galana was more reserved or, perhaps, confused.

Indeed, there was a great deal of confusion. "You are Vasema?" asked Lord Corad.

"So it is, husband-to-be. But you may still call me Sesa. That's what Daddy names me." Now Galana came and also wrapped her arms about her daughter, perhaps with every bit as much passion as her husband, only exhibited less exuberantly.

She is an attractive sort, isn't she? thought Qala. Rather on the large size, though, and certainly a few years older than she. Not the time to think on such things!

It took the afternoon to recount all that had happened, leaving out any references to monsters and gods. They may have left a few gaping holes in their story by so doing.

"Then we *shall* have a wedding at the Yule," finally said Lady Belema. "As near as that is, you might as well stay," she told Vasema's parents.

"Of course, you are invited," she added, addressing Qala.

"That goes without question," stated Vasema. "Also my best friend in the world, Mistress Domi." She giggled. "If her duties as bailiff permit."

"I'll give her the day," Qala said, and drank more of Hurrum's wine. It was the best she had tasted in some time. "And if this Sharshite noble mistreats you, remember you can always have your old job back."

"She's more likely to mistreat him," allowed Lord Vullum.

His wife seemed ready to reprove him but, instead, laughed. "It is so. As long as the willful girl has horses to ride and game to hunt, you can probably keep her happy, Lord Corad."

"Oh, I intend to help manage the estate, too!" proclaimed Vasema. "I have many ideas on agriculture."

"So I know," spoke Corad. "Your spouting of them was one of the first thing to endear you to me."

"A match made by the gods," said Qala, and they would never know how true that was. "To the gods!" She raised her cup. "Every one of them!"

AFTERWORD

I hope you have enjoyed THE CROCODILE'S SON. This is a sequel of sorts to THE EYES OF THE WIND and, as that novel, is set in the world of my DONZALO'S DESTINY sequence, but thirteen or so centuries earlier. The technological level is meant to be similar to that of Late Antiquity or the very beginning of the Medieval period.

The magic, however, is the same. These novels serve as a sort of bridge between my Malvern books and the Donzalo ones, but it is not necessary to read any of those to understand this one. Of course, I hope you will!

Expect to see more of Qala and, of course, her son.

Stephen Brooke

Author Stephen Brooke lives in an old farmhouse in the Florida Panhandle. He is the author of more than twenty books, as well as an artist and musician.

Visit the Arachis Press at http://arachispress.com for more of his work.

www.ingramcontent.com/pod-product-compliance
Lightning Source LLC
Chambersburg PA
CBHW060400030726
47497CB00003B/789